TALONS

Also by Anthony Mancini

MENAGE
THE YELLOW GARDENIA

TALONS

A Novel

Anthony Mancini

DONALD I. FINE, INC.
New York

Copyright © 1991 by Anthony Mancini

Library of Congress Cataloging-in-Publication Data
Mancini, Anthony.
    Talons / by Anthony Mancini.
      p. cm.
    ISBN 1-55611-234-3
    I. Title.
    PS3563.A4354T35   1991
    813'.54—dc20   90-56075
                                          CIP

Manufactured in the United States of America

10 9 8 7 6 5 4 3 2 1

Designed by Irving Perkins Associates

Dedicated to Owen Laster

There, too, flushed Ganymede, his rosy thigh
  Half buried in the eagle's down,
Sole as a flying star shot through the sky
  Above the pillared town.

TENNYSON

FALCONER

One

*Death on wings had come to New York City. But
it began...*

IN THE SPRING in the rugged land of Kirghizia. Spring too
when the winds of death had turned southeast and south,
breathing their venom of cesium isotopes over Central Asia.
Spring not green but black.

Raven Lokka was serving as a diplomatic attaché in
Frunze, capital of the Soviet Republic of Kirghiz on the Chu
River in the foothills of the mottled mountains called the
Ala-Tau. Lokka, an engineer by profession, participated in
a scientific exchange program, advising the Soviet authorities on irrigation projects stemming from the local hydroelectric dam. It was here that his passion for the ancient
art of falconry would be sparked.

The countryside around Frunze reminded the attaché of

3

his native Minnesota, the land dotted with jack pine and teeming with wildlife. On weekends and days off he would backpack to the northern slopes of the Kirghiz range to revel in the splendid savagery of the land and observe the animal life—mouflon, antelope, marmot, yak, wild horse.

On one of these outings he met Ali Kanat.

Ali Kanat was a scar-faced member of a highland tribe of nomads who herded flocks of cattle and sheep to the high pastures in summer and spent the bitter winter in sheltered rifts between the mountains. They lived in villages composed of mud houses with flat roofs thatched with hay. Raven Lokka, stumbling upon the village by chance, was treated with big displays of Moslem hospitality and open-mouthed curiosity by the people who rode small stocky horses and led around two-humped Bactrian camels as pack animals. Ali Kanat, perhaps recognizing a kindred soul in Lokka, sort of adopted him. Lokka's ancestors were Finnish and Ojibwa Indian and maybe the tribesman detected the common Asian bloodlines in both these heritages, linking the attaché somewhere in the dawn of history to himself, a son of Turkic and Mongol ancestors. Or maybe Ali Kanat simply saw in Lokka another votary like himself of the fathomless mysteries of the animal kingdom.

On his subsequent visits to the village the American was gradually inducted by his mentor into the select priesthood of falconry.

Falconry as practiced in Central Asia, if not quite a religion, was more an art form than a sport. The skill had been handed down over the centuries since its invention by the Moghuls of Tartary. Lokka would prove himself an eager and adept student.

Ali Kanat, a nut-brown man with a furrowed face that gave few clues to his age, trained berkute eagles to take quarry as large as wolves and antelopes. The slash marks on his wrist and forearm and the meandering scar on his right cheek served as mementos of mishaps during training the large and powerful raptors. He showed off these connective tissue souvenirs with an air of great pride as if they were medals of honor or proofs of some mystic kinship with the keen-sighted bird of prey whose tearing talons he had felt like a rough kiss on the flesh. He soon infected Lokka with his enthusiasm for falconry.

His practice of falconry required infinite patience and great reserves of empathy for members of the alien species of birds, Lokka soon learned. The Kirghiz hunted with eagles by strapping a large wooden t-pole to the side of a horse where the raptor, far too powerful for perching on the hunter's arm, could stand. Carried otherwise an eagle in *yarak* (Kirghiz for being in top-notch condition primed for the kill) might tense up when sensing the presence of nearby quarry and splinter the falconer's arm. But the danger began when the falconer took the fledgling from the eyrie, risking the anger of the eyass' glaring parents.

Young eagles, nesting in high and inaccessible places, could be captured only during a short period of summer. Reaching them often involved following the trail of the sure-footed mouflon and scaling the sheer face of a cliff. Ali disdained using ladders, pikes, irons and the like, climbing only with his hands and feet and a long length of strong rope. Training the raptor also required skill, patience, and gentleness. The fledgling immediately was equipped with a hood for the head, jesses, swivel, leash and bell. Important as they were, these physical items were not nearly as crucial to the success of training as the falconer's sensitivity to the spirit of the raptor as a feral creature.

Since the behavior of the bird of prey was manipulated through the appetite, Ali Kanat underscored for his American pupil the importance of maintaining the eagle in a perpetual state of natural equilibrium between satiety and hunger, so that when flown to hunt, the berkute would be keen enough to go after food but swift and strong enough to snatch the quarry. It was a neat balancing act of animal management.

"In yarak," Ali Kanat would tell Lokka, who soon had picked up the local dialect, "the berkute manifests the spirit of *Allah* and the balance between mountain and air, bird and quarry, man and beast, body and soul." The tribesman's eyes were intense as he spoke. "It is life eternal frozen in a moment of death."

The bird's victory over the prey was far from a foregone conclusion. In his days as a falconer Ali had lost three eagles to the wolves. He also hand-trapped and trained haggards, adult eagles, and was renowned in the highlands for his genius as a handler of birds. His advice and technique were greatly sought after. Choosing Raven Lokka as his main disciple had kindled much envy among the mountaineers.

Once in the month of April Lokka took a leave of absence from government work to witness Ali Kanat training a haggard named Fatima. Ali carried the eagle on the gauntlet that he wore on his right arm (western falconers carried on the left) with an air of great tenderness and infinite care, as if the bird were his own offspring, the latest in a line of aerial children bred for the field of combat. For many hours at a stretch he would carry the hooded berkute on his fist, making cooing sounds and stroking the bird's head with a feather. This helped habituate the raptor to the presence of men and other animals. The stars over Kirghizia blazed and the moon rose like a pale neon globe over the jagged mountain tops. At night the falconer leashed the blindfolded creature to a perch in a long hut where the windows had been shaded to blot out all possible light. She was prompted to feed by the falconer passing a morsel of hare, rodent, raw beef or lamb across her crooked feet while tickling them with the feather. As the tantalized berkute snapped at the food the falconer managed to place a sliver in her mouth, whistling low as she lodged the food in her crop, repeating the process until very soon the eagle associated the sound of the whistle with the act of eating. It didn't take long for Fatima, a bird of intelligence, to show signs of qualifying as an ace huntress and companion. She would not start any longer at Ali Kanat's growly voice nor flutter her wings in fright when he entered the room. She routinely would climb off the perch when the gloved hand was placed under her feet. Now would begin the gradual process of changing the rufter hood for a more easily fitting one that might be slipped off and on less obtrusively while slowly acclimating the berkute to feeding in the light of day and the presence of men.

The hoods were switched in a velvety dark room. While Ali Kanat worked, Raven Lokka held his breath, but everything went well. Soon Fatima was feeding in a darkened room with her hood off and gradually more and more light was allowed to seep in.

In a few days the bird feasted on carrion in the open air in broad daylight. As children romped and dogs yapped and camels lumbered through the village center, Fatima, sometimes hooded and sometimes not, fed and preened, almost a member of the clan.

"She truly seems a gifted bird," Ali said.

"She'll certainly make a spirited raptor," Lokka said.

"We hope for it," Ali said, "but the day is still a long way off."

Fatima was taken on the fist down the muddy paths of the village, again hooded and unhooded. On the rare occasions when the bird became frightened the falconer would slip the hood back on her head. And Raven Lokka, dressed in sheepskin, always came along, feeling like a novitiate of an exotic priesthood.

The time came to feed Fatima live animals, mice, marmots, baby hares. She was usually left unhooded now, though leashed to the perch in the mews. The next step in training approached quickly—casting her to the lure. The first step was teaching the berkute to respond to the falconer's voice. At his shout the bird was trained in the field to leap to the fist or pole and feed until she associated the act of eating with the distinctive sound of the trainer's voice. Next the falconer introduced the bird to the lure. Ali Kanat used a scrap of fox fur garnished with mutton and tied to a string. The lure was tossed a few feet in front of the unhooded eagle. After feeding on the lure the bird was enticed back to feed out of the falconer's hand as he barked commands in his gritty voice. Fatima was never overfed, was kept sleek and keen on a leash, later on a *creance*, a long fine line attached to the leash and swivel. She was given a longer and longer leash and would strut brazenly around the lure, feeding in the falconer's presence. Day after day the distance to which the lure was thrown was increased. And Raven Lokka, acting as falconer's assistant, would launch each training session by holding and unhooding the berkute while Ali shouted at her and cast the lure into the crystalline air. Lokka had never felt more profoundly alive.

Soon Fatima was voluntarily flying to the lure, ranging to distances of some 250 feet, and Ali's burnished teakwood face was wreathed in a smile that buried the scar.

"Now she is ready," he told Lokka, "to learn to stoop to the lure."

Next morning the falconer strapped the t-pole to his stocky piebald horse and mounted the animal while Raven Lokka carried the hooded bird. When they reached the training field, Lokka unhooded the berkute as usual but this time, after casting out the lure and shouting, the falconer snatched the meat away at the last second, causing the eagle to overfly the mark. This was repeated until the creature began to learn to search for the decoy, to stoop backward and forward to snatch her prize.

Finally one morning Ali announced that Fatima was ready to be introduced to the hunt, to take live quarry.

In only a few days Lokka had to return to Frunze for reassignment back to the States. He had been waiting expectantly for this moment.

Ali looked solemn. "It's risky," he said. "She is a wild-caught passage bird. If we unleash her she may never return to us."

Lokka was given a blanket and a mount. The day was clear and beautiful. Wildflowers sprouted in the meadows and crags. Majestic clouds rolled along in an azure sky. Fatima rode unhooded on the t-pole, a queen in a sedan chair. Her jesses were leashless. When they reached an area that the falconer's sharp senses told him was teeming with quarry, Ali cast off the regal buteo, who with a tingling of bells soared off into the sky.

Fatima, following quarry over open country, struck often and struck well and always returned to the pole. Soon she had captured two hares and a marmot that were placed in Ali's rawhide sidebags. The most breathtaking moment, though, came as the sun was setting and Fatima took her first wolf.

Actually it was Ali, eagle-eyed himself, who first spotted the animal with the shaggy brown coat and erect ears slinking across a gully. As if telepathically sensing the falconer's awareness of the quarry's presence, Fatima rose from the pole and sailed at low altitude toward the wolf.

The wolf had no chance as the eagle slammed from a high stoop into her crouching prey, combining physical mass and blinkering speed behind such elastic talons. The immobilized animal lay helpless under the broad-winged bird, who bound the wolf's spine, then, as the wolf turned its head to try to bite the raptor, bound the nose, suffocating the victim. The kill was accomplished in less than three minutes.

On the day before Lokka was scheduled to leave, the falconer disappeared for the entire day, then returned after sundown looking weary and carrying an osier hamper filled with straw. And in the lidded hamper was the frightened eyass of wild berkutes. Ali had climbed a mountain to steal her from the nest.

"I trapped her where the Chu flows north on the western slopes of the Kunghei Ala-Tau," Ali said. "I believe, my friend, that she will grow to be a great bird and that you, Raven Lokka, are destined to become a great falconer."

FOUR days later Lokka smuggled the eyass back to the States in a military transport plane. There was no time to go through channels and apply for a license. The eagle's training had to begin immediately, while she was still in her infancy, or she would never become fused to the falconer's will. This fledgling was unusually large, and Lokka wondered about this. In his present mood, fresh from the mysticism of his time with Ali, he smiled to himself and wondered if it were some omen that here was a noble bird and he was, as Ali said, somehow destined to become a great falconer.

At Dover Air Force Base, sipping whiskey in the Officers Club, he thought about what name to give the bird, which came from the arid lands where Tamerlane had constructed pyramids of human skulls, where the Hunnish hordes originated. Drawing on childhood memories of his father reading him the Scandinavian sagas and his college studies of the *Nibelungenlied*, he decided to call her Brunhild, sister of Attila, rival of Gudrun. It certainly seemed a fitting name for such a promisingly mighty female bird of prey.

Lokka returned to Minnesota on furlough from the State

Department on July 1, 1986. Ali Kanat had given him the fledgling on June 20, 1986. The bird had been born about ten days earlier. That meant that her parents had mated about forty days before her birth, near the first of May, about a week after a staggering disaster had occurred in another part of the Soviet Union.

The mating of eagles, Ali had told Lokka, was a graceful, beautiful spectacle. The male performed a spiraling dance in the air, fluttering slotted wings. The female in her eyrie would spot him and take off in pursuit. They would glide together in ever-smaller circles, ascending into the sky. Then at a mysteriously preordained moment the mating birds would clasp each other's talons and swirl to earth to consummate the union.

In such fashion Brunhild's parents performed their ballet of procreation. But their dance of life was done on winds of death flowing over their wings, winds that had come from far away in the Ukraine, from a power station located at the settlement of Pripyat, ten miles northwest of the city of Chernobyl.

Two

RAVEN LOKKA MET Iris Frazier soon after he returned to his family house on the lip of Lake Superior in north Minnesota. It was a happy time for him, becoming a falconer and courting his future wife.

Iris' geranium-petal sort of beauty had attracted Lokka when he first saw her in the bookstacks of the town library. Before Iris he had always favored outdoorsy women with big voices and lusty appetites. Iris was different, well-named, slender with slanting tawny eyes and honey-colored hair. She had a kind of diaphanous, near-spiritual quality. She taught at the local high school, not exactly a spiritual experience, and wrote poetry.

Lokka had been looking for a book on Jaeger, the German falconer, when he brushed past her near the biography shelves. She smiled at him. One thing led to another and they had coffee and croissants at a little place overlooking the harbor. It was mid-July and the lake was scalloped with white sails. Gulls swooped and squawked over the sun-sequined water. She wore a candy-striped silk shirt. Her hair was cropped in West Bank bohemianism. In spite of the otherwise mannish touches, she radiated femininity and showed a lot of curiosity about him. Everybody knew every-body else in town and his was an unfamiliar face to her. She had come to live there from the western part of the state after Lokka had left for the Soviet Union. In any case, his lone-wolf ways made him sort of a curiosity to most residents and a figure of mystery to those who happened to have known his family and were aware of his existence. He was the only child of parents who had died many years earlier. As a half-breed Lokka, though not quite a pariah, lived out of the mainstream of community life in a place where for the most part people kept to themselves.

Somehow Iris inspired the normally uncommunicative engineer to open up and tell her about his experiences in Kirghizia and how he had just begun to train an outlaw bird to the lure.

Which immediately sparked her interest. She asked him question after question about falconry. It had been a long time since he met someone he felt so comfortable with. Through her eyes he began to see himself and his activities with a new appreciation and enthusiasm. She smelled of jasmine. He began to pour out his thoughts and feelings to her like hoarded wine into a cup. She brought him out of his shell. Before parting they made a date to attend a concert in Grand Portage the next week.

In these days he kept Brunhild in the shed behind the house, a long narrow building, shaded by maples and pines, that made an ideal mews. The hamper was attached to a beam a few feet off the ground. Lokka fed the fledgling well and often on fresh-killed game, fowl, and rabbits. The food was placed on the lid of the hamper and tied to a wooden block. Lokka would be as unobtrusive in the shed as possible, entering quietly, leaving the food and withdrawing quickly. The more free and feral the eyass was during the time of "hack," the better huntress she would turn out to be.

As summer wore on Brunhild began to venture outside, perching on the roof of the shed and the limbs of decaying tree trunks. In late August when she was about ten weeks old she was fully fledged and ready to fly. Her tarsal feathers were light red and her tail banded with white at the base. She tested her wings over the surrounding countryside, gradually extending her range. But she would always return to the feeding place. Soon she was preying on mice, and Lokka decided it was time to rig her with jesses, swivel, leash and bell and acquaint her with the lure.

At the same time he conducted a whirlwind courtship of Iris Frazier. Having escaped a straightlaced upbringing as a Lutheran minister's daughter in Willmar in the western section of the state, she was especially drawn to what she perceived as Lokka's unconventional, free-spirited way of life. On his side Lokka was attracted by her direct and trusting personality. A good match. They were married in November by a justice-of-the-peace in a five-minute ceremony during a weekend trip to the Isle Royale National Park, their honeymoon a two-day canoe trip up the Pigeon River. By the time they returned to the lakeside house Iris Frazier Lokka was pregnant.

Meanwhile her husband continued to train the growing raptor. Brunhild rebelled at the jesses and bell. One time she did not return to the hack for her meal, and Lokka worried that he had lost her for good. But in a few hours she returned and Lokka snared her in a bow-net and grounded her for a while to teach her a lesson. It was evident to him that she was a spirited bird with a streak of roguishness and independence. In fact, she had the ideal personality for an eagle destined to become a formidable predator. And she was larger than any eaglet he had ever seen. In fact her tail already measured some three feet and her wing-chord six. Lokka decided he now had to prove himself by dominating this mutinous if obviously talented bird.

From late fall till February Brunhild spent most of the time roosting in the shed. From time to time Lokka took her out to train to the lure in open fields under the pale winter sky. Prey was scarce, but left to her own devices she often took mice and small rabbits. She always returned to Lokka's voice and the lure, but did not seem at all submissive or tame. Rather she gave the distinct impression that if she returned and went through her paces as a falconer's bird she did so of her own free will and that one day she might assert her independence. She was a beast to be reckoned with, which excited Lokka. More, he realized that in a way he was beginning to love the raptor.

Lokka had received the news of his wife's pregnancy with a sense of awe, but it didn't last . . . he was too wrapped up in training Brunhild and studying Jaeger's theories of falconry. He realized that Iris was beginning to be disenchanted with his obsession, but did not handle the problem very well.

One evening, sitting by the fireplace, she said, "Isn't it just my luck to have as a rival a female who belongs to a different species."

He frowned at the tumbler of whiskey he had been nursing, then looked up at her. "Well, at least you won't catch us screwing." He forced a smile.

"I'm not so sure of that. Didn't I read somewhere that the vulture goddesses of ancient Egypt took human form?" She smiled back at him.

There followed a truce, or perhaps a stand-off.

CAME spring, the season when prey foraging for their young became more vulnerable. Lokka took Brunhild out to the field to teach her to wait on the lure. In a wide open space he turned her loose from the fist into a pastel sky. He wore a leather gauntlet that he had bought in a hardware store. She was large enough now that such precautions had to be taken. Soon, he figured, he would have to buy a fencing mask to protect his eyes and face from her talons. She circled now, expecting him to hurl the lure. Instead he prepared to release one young rabbit from a knitting basket that he had brought along. He waited till the eagle had climbed higher than usual and her head was turned in toward him before setting the rabbit free.

Brunhild struck. The first rabbit killed, the raptor mounted the pink morning sky to wait on the next. He released another with the same result. He allowed her to feed a little before calling her off. She did not carry; she did not disobey. He was pleased. She seemed to be in yarak, eager to take wild game.

That day she took two snakes, a tree squirrel, and a musk-rat, soaring in broad-winged flight and gliding down to snatch up the quarry by surprise. Lokka rewarded her with some prime beefsteak, satisfied with the way she was progressing but wanting to fly her at larger game.

Timberwolves. The wolves of the steppes of Central Asia slinked across her genetic history. Such quarry was her birth-right, and Lokka felt he was ready to apply the training techniques he had learned from studying Jaeger. He had to be very circumspect, though. If the federal rangers heard about his activities there would be hell to pay.

A week later he hired two Ojibwa boys from the White-face River Reservation. The boys, Jacqui and Pony, were eleven years old and small compared to white youngsters their age. They had even dispositions and learned quickly. Both seemed fearless about what they had to do—act as live bait for a powerful talon-baring raptor.

Iris looked on all this with a mix of horror and fascination, and took refuge in the feelings and physical changes of her pregnancy. She planted a vegetable and flower garden on the side of the house that faced south and was protected from the severe weather spawned by the lake. She stripped paint from wooden furniture. She tried to keep her mind and body occupied, but her fears grew as her belly blossomed.

Meanwhile, her husband lived for hawking...On the morning when he first brought the boys out to the training field the earth chattered and pulsed with life, the sun a firegod resurrected over the lake. He outfitted Pony and Jacqui with strips of protective leather, clothed them in wolfskin and tied raw meat to their backs. They trotted off into the woods. After the boys had gotten a good head start Lokka cast off the raptor from the gloved fist. With a mighty downstroke she sailed into the sky.

Brunhild first caught Pony, slamming him to the ground and mantling her wings over the boy under the protective covering.

Lokka cupped his mouth with two hands and called the bird off. She returned to the fist, gobbling a hunk of meat into her crop, gazing with agate eyes into the distance.

Lokka cast her off again, and within minutes she caught up with Jacqui and knocked him to the earth. Quickly the falconer called her off again and rewarded her with another morsel. Considering the bird's obvious appetite, Lokka reflected that before long she would be ready to take on real wolves.

Two weeks passed, the training was going well, the marriage was not. He berated himself for ignoring Iris, for indulging his obsession to such extremes, and promised to do something about it. That night they made love for the first time in weeks. Afterward he dreamt that his wife delivered a baby wolf.

★ ★ ★

TALONS

THE accident occurred the next day, a foggy May morning, during training, and marked a turning point in Brunhild's development.

He saw the boy Pony stumble over a rock and fall hands first to the ground. The wolfskin flew off his body, exposing a section of shoulder where the leather covering had been torn loose. Talons penetrated flesh.

Lokka, angry and terrified, shouted the bird off, but for a moment the rebel eagle ignored the call. He shouted again. A clash of wills, falconer versus eagle. Suddenly Brunhild returned to the fist.

Only a few seconds had passed, but when it was over the raptor had, for the first time, tasted human flesh.

Iris had thought they should take the boy to the doctor, but the boy insisted he go back to his family, to the Chippewa Reservation, where he would, he said, be taken care of. Raven was ashamed to realize he was relieved— if the boy had been taken to the local doctor his illegal falconry would become known and he might well be stopped. Iris cleansed and dressed the puncture wound, shaking her head, and Raven drove the boys back to the Reservation, giving each a fifty-dollar bonus. He never saw them again.

"I'M scared, Raven," Iris announced after he returned home.

"Of what?" Though of course he knew.

"I'm scared for you, for me, for our baby—"

"Scared of *what?*" Defensively.

"You know what."

"Iris, she's only a bird—"

"Only a bird? That's right. But a bird right out of hell."

"Don't be melodramatic." But to himself he acknowledged that there was indeed something otherworldly, if not hellish, about the bird. Which, God help him, only enhanced the fascination.

Iris reached to him and clasped his hand. *"Let her go, Raven. Please."*

"What?"

"Release her to the wild."

Lokka glanced at the mahogany bar, at the brightly colored lanterns that swayed over the sawdust-covered plank floor.

"I can't," he said.

JACK started life on August 11, 1987, after Brunhild had entered her second year. A rather puny baby, he tipped the scales at only five pounds at birth. The raptor, meanwhile, had grown to a prodigious size, weighing some twenty-two pounds and having a wingspan of over ten feet. Lokka had never heard of a golden eagle achieving such size, especially not an immature one. By this time she was attacking and killing wolves, and Lokka mused that it would not surprise him if she next began to prey on bears.

As autumn approached Lokka worried that the eagle might return to the wild on her own, spurred by the mysterious migratory instinct. But Brunhild, newly fledged after spending a lazy summer molting in the mews, did not abandon him. He wondered if she had formed as strong an attachment to him as he had to her. He kept her in the best possible health during her second winter, feeding her fresh pigeons, beefsteak, rabbits, and following Ali's teachings he also gave her poultry castings—wings, heads and necks—with the blood removed. Tearing the pinion joints of fowl and biting bones provided her with good exercise and kept her beak in good shape. He kept her in the shed or tethered to a large block of wood on the lawn behind the house. She perched on the branches of dead tree trunks and bathed in a large old slop sink Lokka had provided. He treated her like a feathered queen, although she seemed to treat her master with regal disdain.

Was he really her master?

When he approached her in the shed or on the lawn she never beat her wings, showing eagerness to hop to his fist in the way he had seen birds behave with Ali. She would answer his call, but always, he thought, with a certain air of *noblesse oblige*. She seemed to have a definite sense of her own importance. He kept her crop full all winter and they seldom hunted. Prey was scarce in any case. Still, he tried to take her out every day to exercise her wings.

Iris, who had called herself the bird's rival, began to see more of her husband. As, of course, did the baby. Lokka, after an early and odd indifference, found himself growing fond of this frail and pale changeling he had fathered. Jack had very light milky-gray eyes and blond down covering his melonlike skull. He was a precocious smiler who bawled very little. He would coo and kick his dimpled legs whenever Lokka came close to him. On the rare occasions when he cried he would stop if his father entered the room and puckered his face with pleasure when Raven kissed him.

Iris noted with pleasure the bond growing between father and son. Obviously she hoped that the relationship would begin to overshadow her husband's mania for the bird, which she was beginning to regard as a sort of bedevilment. Maybe paternal love would provide the exorcism. The atmosphere in the house that winter brimmed with health and wholesomeness—she breast-fed the boy and baked ginger cookies; the aroma of cedar burning in the fireplaces filled the rooms; Raven whittled toy soldiers and brought home fish from the lake.

Brunhild roosted in the shed.

Lokka supplemented their income by selling fish and game to campers and townspeople. They had enough money

20

in savings to get by for a year or so. Iris raised the possibility of her returning to teaching school.

Raven vetoed the idea. "Jack needs you," he said.

She did not argue with him.

Then came the spring of 1988.

Lokka burned to return to the hunt. It was like an addiction. He could not really explain it. Springtime, the earth's juices flowed, the land teemed with prey. Lokka put on the leather gauntlet and fencing mask and resumed the affair with Brunhild.

Toward the end of May he had been flying the eagle at timberwolves in the foothills of the Sawtooth Mountains. No luck. At one point, as the raptor was soaring free, the falconer lost sight of her. This happened often enough not to make him too worried. She was conditioned to returning to his yell sooner or later. Feeling tired, he took off his equipment and lay down on a boulder to snooze and sunbathe. Just as the gauze of sleep was netting his eyes he was startled to wakefulness by an alarming cry.

He got to his feet and rushed in the general direction of the commotion. Reaching the edge of a ravine, he parted the branches of a balsam, and what he saw in the distance made him catch his breath. A campsite beside a frothy stream. On a bright red tarp the bloody carcass of a deer. A hunter in a yellow slicker holding his shoulder stained with blood. Another man aiming a rifle at the broad-winged form of the great berkute lifting off into the sky.

The rifle cracked twice, the shooter let the weapon dangle from one hand as he shaded his eyes with the other. He had missed.

Lokka ran back to the boulder and hallooed. Quickly Brunhild returned to the fist. He tethered her and hurried back to the land rover.

* * *

THE next day Lokka made a point of driving to town on the pretext of buying groceries, picked up a newspaper and thumbed through for a while before he found the item— two deer hunters from Des Moines reported having been attacked by a large bird. One was treated for a serious shoulder wound. They said the creature had resembled a "giant vulture" of some kind. The writer handled the account in a dry, skeptical way. City slickers, the thinking was. Couldn't tell a vulture from a meadowlark. Probably stabbed himself with his Hammacher Schlemmer Swiss army knife.

Lokka tossed the newspaper into a trash basket and walked back across the mall parking lot to the land rover. What to do? Maybe Iris was right, maybe he should give up the bird. As he drove back to the house he went to the brink of setting her free, then thought of Ali Kanat and the time in the mountains of Kirghizia. He began to persuade himself that the incident with the hunters had been an aberration, but then he recalled what had happened to Pony and he wavered again.

He did nothing. He told Iris nothing about the incident, though she sensed that something was wrong...

Jack grew bigger and stronger. He went off the breast and began eating solid food. He googled sounds approximating words and sentences. He crawled, then took stumbling steps as he held onto furniture. He was changing from a baby into a toddler. Raven's interest in his son was renewed. As the weather improved he took the boy outdoors to play with a rubber ball. In June, when he was ten months old, Jack began to walk without holding onto anything. He was still small for his age but seemed advanced in the so-called motor skills and very agile...

One morning under a hot pearl sky Jack laughed uproariously as his father carried him piggyback, circling the house and whooping like a wild Indian. The eagle seemed to glare at them from the dark recesses of the shed. What of it? thought Lokka, catching sight of Brunhild. Eagles always glared. It was their only facial expression. He had not flown her for weeks. Who knew, maybe he would never fly her again? He continued to romp with his son.

Two days later: dusk. In the backyard Lokka reclined against a tree trunk and watched Jack chase fireflies. The boy trailed behind him a stuffed rabbit. Iris was on the front porch swing.

The bird appeared out of nowhere and slammed the child to the ground.

In an instant Raven was on his feet and had grabbed a garden rake lying nearby. Jack bawled. Before the bird could sink her talons into the child, Lokka was there swinging the rake.

She flew off into the dusky summer sky.

Iris, who had heard the commotion from the front porch, scooped the child up in her arms and pressed him close. Staring into his tear-stained red face she hurriedly patted all over his body, searching for wounds.

Lokka examined the boy too. "He's okay." Frowning at the sky he added, "Thank heaven."

Iris said, "Please, Raven, don't let her come back, don't let her *ever* come back."

Brunhild, tied to a long leash attached to a block of wood, had to be perched somewhere nearby. Raven, heart thudding, took an instant to make up his mind. He walked over to the block of wood, untied the leash, then with perspiring hands, threw it into the tall grass.

Iris, holding the child tight, said nothing but gazed at her husband with a mixture of relief and satisfaction.

Lokka did not look at his wife or son. His misty gray eyes were too busy scanning the brilliant summer sky.

Three

TWICE THE BERKUTE tried to return to the shed, but Lokka managed to chase her off with the rake, each time a wrenching experience for him.

He could not identify it, but something inside Lokka rebelled at severing the connection with the bird. No experience of his life had equalled in intensity and pure joy the days of hawking. He could not find the words to describe the sense of oneness, the dissolution of self that had marked the episodes of falconry. A piece of him always ached to recapture those moments.

Even after the unspeakable events that would soon follow his setting her free.

Two months passed.

Dawn. From the lake, the skittish flight of mallards. In the distance, the thunder of a herd of elk.

Lokka was awakened by the reveille of instinct. Buck naked, he tumbled out of bed and groped in the waning darkness toward the front porch. Gray eyes scanned the murky water mirroring the piney bluffs above the house. He found a pack of cigarettes on the cane side table and lit one. The tip glowed. As he searched the glacial waters of Lake Superior fear grew. Wind rustled the reeds at the edge of the lake. Something was wrong, his old bloodlines told him. Something terribly wrong. His eyes lifted to the sky.

The moon lingered in the burnt-rose canopy of the late August dawn. The previous evening in the same patch of sky he had traced the constellation Aquila and, in his fashion, took it as a sign. Plumes of his cigarette smoke rose on the thermals of the summer air.

Air.

High in the atmosphere she soared, lengthening her grandiose wings to the fullest. She flew west from the direction of Eagle River over the waving surface of the lake toward the peaks of the Sawtooth Mountains. Scooping pockets of precious air along her wing tips, she glided toward the destination. Toward quarry.

In the updraft, the tail fanned out. She swiveled her fearsome head from side to side, beak clicking. The rising sun glinted off her golden hackles as she approached the western shoreline. Soon she shifted the camber of her wings and stooped to earth—toward the house ...

In the house overlooking the lake he squashed out the cigarette in a clam ashtray. A breeze rose, similar to the breeze that crossed the portages of the old explorers and fur traders, and caressed his unclothed body, ruffled the curtains of the screened porch. His body tensed. Why did he wake up? he wondered. What sparked this instinct of danger? He waited, listened.

The breeze also swayed the hammock where the child slept in the open-air back porch. He wore red cotton pajamas and a look of utter peacefulness. The mosquito netting had fallen to the floor. He clasped to his gently heaving chest the stuffed gray rabbit...

On another current of air the bird banked and dove, taut as a crossbow, wing tips pulled back to reduce lift, tail braking. Soon the tail too was pulled back for the final dive. All the while her suprasensory eyes fastened onto the distant daub of red on the back porch. She brought into position the landing gear—her large, powerful talons.

The man on the front porch sensed her nearness. He stiffened. He heard the bells.

The sound came from the back porch. Then he realized the boy was sleeping outside to escape the heat of the house. In a flash he realized what might happen. Still naked, he hurtled out the screen door and ran toward the rear of the house.

At impact her legs were extended to their utmost, her head bent into her crop. She quickly bound to her defenseless prey and mantled him in triumph, then took his thigh in the steel grip of her claws. Raising her wings and slotting the external primaries, she took off into the wind.

Lokka arrived too late. He looked up and, just as he feared, saw her, dropping slightly in altitude, then lifting again to glide out over the lake. Dimly he made out the child's body dangling like a rag doll from her left foot.

Raven Lokka raised two clenched fists to the heavens and let out a long, unearthly scream.

QUARRY

Four

ANTONIA MEADOWS DESCENDED the steps just inside the stone wall that surrounded Central Park. She looked up at the Arsenal, its brick front veiled in ivy. The building, with rifle-shaped balusters on the exterior staircase, white-washed metal doors surrounded by replicas of spears, swords and cannonballs, matched her hostile mood. The doors were surmounted by the effigy of an eagle painted gold.

She entered the Administration Headquarters of the Department of Parks of the City of New York, where she served as Curator of Birds at the Central Park Zoo. In her high-ceilinged private office she raised the venetian blinds with a clatter and winced at the stack of Monday morning paperwork on her desk.

Fillipina Lopez brought her steaming black coffee in a crockery mug inscribed with the words, "I Love New York." "Morning," said the assistant, who was the source of her boss' black mood because last week she had sent a for-your-eyes-only memo meant for the Department of Interior to the state conservation people. Today Antonia had to find a way to dig herself out of that one.

Antonia grumped in reply and removed her hat, a butterfly emerging from a dusty sand-color chrysalis. Antonia Meadows, ornithologist, was herself a rare bird—a beautiful and artlessly stylish woman—chestnut curls, an oval face with small harmonious features, sea-green eyes that shone with intelligence, a long white neck leading to the lithe curves. She looked taller than her five-feet-six inches and younger than her thirty-three years. In the academic and scientific circles in which she traveled she made more heads turn than a flock of barn owls.

Today she wore a cropped glen plaid jacket over a white crepe blouse and a green flannel pleated skirt. Small gold scallop shells adorned her ear lobes.

Behind the façade lay an equally impressive mind—a Phi Beta Kappa from Radcliffe, a masters in biology from Cornell, a doctorate in zoology from Cambridge where she read a paper on the ostrichlike rheas of South America. Formerly married to an eminent New York neurosurgeon twelve years her senior, she held state commendations for her work in rescuing, banding, and studying endangered peregrines. On her part she most prized her baby boy and whittling her post-divorce golf handicap to a lean mean ten. She had, one might say, the whole package. Egg in her beer.

Antonia, however, felt that the whole of her amounted to somewhat less than the sum of her parts. She once acknowledged the description that she was a mix of fire and ice, but that neither character trait had gained ascendancy. So she was kind of in imbalance, she thought. But she was working on it.

Fillipina handed over a sheaf of phone messages.

"Mr. Marburg called from the main office."

Antonia grimaced. What did the General Curator want this early on a Monday morning?

Fillipina, a small woman with frazzled red hair and the soul of a victim, seemed to read Antonia's mind. "He must've been up with the chickens."

The ornithologist wondered briefly whether the remark had been made on purpose—Al Marburg, an expert in mammals, had a decidedly bantam strut. No, irony was not one of Fillipina's strong points.

Glancing at the other messages, most of which had been left over from Friday afternoon, Antonia said, "Ring him back for me, will you please?"

Sipping coffee, Antonia scanned the newspaper while mentally planning her day. She was not exactly swamped with zoo-related work this time of year although she had plenty to do in connection with the courses she taught in natural history at the Graduate Center. Then there was her social life with Joe Bannister, her fiancé and press secretary to the Mayor of New York City. As the desk calendar leaf featuring the head of a polar bear indicated, she was scheduled to accompany him this evening to a fund-raising cocktail party for the Municipal Art Society and to a screening Wednesday of a film shot in New York the previous spring with the close cooperation of the Mayor's office. Which meant two nights at least when she would have to smooth things over with her son Guy. Her son was three years old now, and she knew she was missing too much of the quicksilver excitement of his growing up. She often physically ached to be with him, but there was no getting around it— she loved her work with a passion that rivaled her maternal feelings. No matter what the pop psychologists tried to peddle, Antonia knew, a woman could not have it all.

Still, she fretted over it, wondering if it was a case of daughter emulating parents.

Ford Meadows had been what they used to call a country gentleman, an untitled baron of the Connecticut River Valley who grew tobacco for a living and killed ducks for sport. He was Antonia's first and formative obsession. Undoubtedly he had bequeathed her the profound interest in animals and nature's handiwork. He also gave her a certain flintiness that she recognized and that troubled her in private moments.

Her mother Pauline Alban Meadows, while she showed no particular kinship for the so-called lower animals, had a lively if mercurial interest in certain bipeds, especially some whose hair was brilliantined, whose features were carved from weathered wood and who often carried tennis rackets or cocktail glasses. While she pursued these interests her husband conveniently looked the other way. She was a woman of volcanic passions, quick to erupt, then lay dormant for long periods. From her Antonia probably got her short fuse and the intensity of feeling she lavished on her work and in her better moments on her son.

The telephone console chirped. She picked up the receiver. "Al?"

"No, it's me," came Fillipina's scratchy voice. "I have Mr. Bannister on the line."

"What happened to Marburg?"

"I can't get through."

"Keep trying. Put Joe on."

Waiting for Joe Bannister's resonant baritone, she glanced at a Japanese painting on the wall of a goshawk preening its feathers.

She heard heavy breathing.

"Come on, Joe. Cut it out."

"Quick, describe what you're wearing."

"A Mother Hubbard and combat boots." And couldn't help laughing. Joe, in many ways an eight-by-ten glossy, did

32

manage to bring her out of herself at times. And, superficial as he might be, she needed that. Well, didn't she?

"Remember, we have a date tonight," he said.

"Is that what you call it? Me standing around with a plastic glass of flat champagne and a plastic smile while you work the room, buttering power brokers from here to Kew Gardens?"

"Sacrifices must be made."

"Sure. Now is the time for all good men to come to the aid of their party."

Okay, he was ambitious, a climber, some might say, but at least he didn't delude himself. In a way she admired how he made no bones about his ambition. And he wasn't the type to play it safe. She also appreciated it that he spared her any phony speeches about the public weal. His motives were self-serving, but in case they helped somebody else along the way, okay, that was a plus. He was, thankfully, *never* pompous, unlike so many other political operatives.

"What time, Joe?" she asked, noticing that her number-two line was flashing. Must be Marburg.

"Eight. On the nose, eh?"

"I'll try. Gotta run, another call." She pressed the button. "Yes?"

"It's Marburg," said Fillipina, "and he sounds real steamed."

What the hell was bugging the Mammal Man? She shrugged. The little rooster didn't scare her. She depressed the phone button. "Hello, Al. What's up?"

"We're meeting in the Temperate Zone in fifteen minutes, all the execs. At the panda exhibit." He was breathing heavily.

"What's wrong?"

"You'll find out when you get there." A muffled voice in the background. "Take a message," Marburg said to his secretary. "I'm in conference. I'll be in conference for the rest of the morning, except to the Commissioner. Oh," and then to Antonia, "Gotta hang up, it's the Commissioner."

What was wrong? Al Marburg might be a fatuous fool, but hardly an alarmist. It had to be something pretty important to lure him away from the log fire in his wonderful landmark office into the city's winter chill.

THE scientific name for the animal was *Ailurus fulgens*. The Sherpas of the Himalayan foothills, source of the animal's bloodline, where farmers cultivated the soil by hand because they believe in the sanctity of beasts, called the species *wah*. In the West it was commonly called the red panda.

Naturalists argued about whether it was more closely related to the bear or the raccoon. They also debated its kinship to the black-and-white giant panda, an Asian neighbor. A crepuscular forager, the red panda preferred a vegetarian diet of bamboo shoots, nuts, fruit and grass. It had a big head, stubby neck, supple torso and a long rusty brush of a tail with dark rings around it. The paws were shod in fluffy brown booties with white soles. The face looked like the invention of a pawky greeting-card illustrator—elfin ears, round visage, white muzzle, molten, friendly eyes. In the wild the red panda was becoming more and more isolated and rare as farms, grazing animals, deforestation and other encroachments shrank its highland habitats. And so it had been labeled by international agreement an endangered species.

New York's Central Park Zoo, though relatively small, boasted two of the furry butterball crowd-pleasers, named Lucy and Desi, penned behind a low wooden fence under an open sky in the so-called Temperate Zone, where they nested in hollow trees, prowled the shrubbery and preened before tourists' video cameras.

But on this bitter February morning Desi lay dead still on the frozen ground, his breast, heart, and lungs torn to shreds. Lucy, his mate, cowered nearby under a hollow log. The animal's lifeless body was circled by six pairs of feet attached to six somber and astonished zoo and park employees.

"Well," said Al Marburg, breaking the sepulchral silence, "what do you all make of it?" He surveyed the circle of stricken faces.

"Could his girl friend have done it?" suggested a florid-faced man in a beaverskin hat and cashmere coat who, looking around, noticed the scornful glances of his colleagues and lapsed into sheepish silence.

"Not likely," said mammal expert Marburg to Ray Kelly, Public Affairs Director of the Parks Department, the only member of the group who was neither a keeper nor a zoologist. The others might forgive his ignorance but would never condone the animal-skin hat. "She's mostly a *folivore* and only infrequently a *carnivore*. She'll eat a mouse now and then when she gets lucky. Her teeth are designed for crushing leaves and that's about it. She's got no carnassial shear."

"Come again?" said Kelly.

"That's the meat-cutting instrument found in the mouths of most carnivores." With two fingers Marburg imitated a scissors. "It's formed by the last upper premolar and the first lower one."

"Sure," said Kelly, blowing on his gloveless hands and stamping the ground.

Bill Frederick (Reptiles) dropped to one knee and focused on the wounds close-up. Parasites were scurrying to the banquet. He slowly shook his shaggy, hatless head. "These wounds don't look like they were caused by teeth," he said. "It almost seems as if the innards were scooped out by... I don't know, something like a sharp-clawed gardening tool."

"Who the hell would do such a thing?" Jane Hellman, Curator of Exhibits, turned to Antonia, who burrowed her pale face into her coat collar.

Marburg fixed his gaze on a shy, nervous youngster who looked more like a boy scout than a zookeeper in the ranger uniform. "When you found him," Marburg asked, "did you notice anything unusual? Anything at all?"

The keeper shrugged, shook his head. "Not a thing. I came to give them a special treat—mulberries I'd defrosted. Look, anybody could've hopped over that fence." He shook his head again. He looked genuinely grief-stricken.

"Got any theories?" Marburg asked Antonia.

She had none.

"Okay," Marburg said, surveying the desolate zoo grounds and the roped-off wooden walkway leading to the panda exhibit, "Jimmy, you stay here and make sure nobody comes within twenty feet of this area. Any problems, use the squawk box."

"Right," the keeper said, sketching some kind of salute.

"How do I handle the press?" asked Kelly.

"You don't. They're not going to hear about it." Marburg inventoried faces. "Are they, folks?"

"So mum's the word, but what are you going to do?" Antonia asked Marburg.

Marburg looked down at the shell of the animal. "What does one do when a rare and valuable thing is brutally and mysteriously destroyed?" Thrusting his pudgy hands in his pockets and walking away, he answered himself: "Call the cops."

Five

LIEUTENANT DAVID TORINO's flesh was in the squad room but his spirits still soared with the condors above the bread-brown volcanic earth and meandering rivers of Patagonia, from where he had returned the previous night after a splendid four-week vacation. The Exec of the NYPD's Major Case Squad shuffled papers around, took a couple of phone calls and tried without success to read a long and tangled internal memo from the Chief of Detectives' staff on the latest uses of computer technology and genetic tests in forensic investigations.

Torino sighed, put aside the report and sipped from a paper cup of orange juice. It was no use, he couldn't get his stylus back into the groove.

The sad-eyed, rawboned cop stretched and daydreamed about his recent travels at the bottom of the earth, where a person still could cross fifty miles of terrain without seeing even one spoor of so-called civilized man, where neither telephone pole nor discarded beer can disfigured the sweeping expanse of sculpted tableland ranged by guanaco and hare, where one could scoop handfuls of water from glacial streams and drink without fear. How long would the place remain unspoiled? he wondered. How long before the stench of sewage displaced the odor of flowers, the blare of car horns drowned out the roar of cataracts and billboards blocked the views of the crests of the cordilleras?

He gazed out the window at the snowcapped peaks of the Municipal Building and asked himself how and when a cop like David Torino gained this uncommon reverence for the earth, and concluded that mostly it derived from his days as an Air Force pilot when he routinely saw the planet from the vantage of an angel, grasping at once its fragile beauty and the vanity of man's constructions. Sure, he thought, we need hydroelectric dams and housing projects. But did we need so many nuclear power plants and ocean-front condos?

He peered again through high-powered eyeglasses at the turgid report. Weak eyesight was why he had resigned from the Air Force to pursue a second career in police work. It was quite a switch, in spite of military similarities. In flight he had found inner peace and an oddly solacing sense of his own insignificance as he glimpsed eternity in the celestial vault and polar lights. Having his wings clipped, though, put him back in the position where the petty concerns of people were magnified, especially in police work, where a purse-snatch was a significant event. He crushed the empty paper cup in his fist and tossed it in the wastepaper basket.

What had attracted Torino, who had majored in philosophy at Columbia College, to a career as a cop? Dementia, he decided. Plus family history and a skewed instinct for reform. Two of his five uncles had been cops. Besides, what else could you do with lousy eyesight and a degree in philosophy?

Still trying to focus on reading while his mind wandered,

Torino brushed back curly brown hair containing too many gray strands for his thirty-eight years. He had an angular face with an aquiline profile, his most outstanding features being extra-large eyelashes.

A waving hand appeared before him.

"Earth to Torino," said the hand's owner, Captain Lee Goldschlager, his superior officer.

"Oh, hi, Lee, what's up?"

"Your head, it's up in the clouds."

Goldschlager, a short-timer counting the ticks to retirement, considered every case a buck to be passed. He held in his beefy hand a faxed memo from the Commissioner's Office. "Got a squeal for yuh."

"From upstairs?"

"A contract. A sensitive matter involving city property."

"Theft?"

"Murder."

Torino made a face. "That's for homicide."

"Hold your water. This isn't homicide. It's pandacide."

"Say what?"

"Right up your alley, animal lover," said Goldschlager, flipping the memo on his subordinate's desk and walking away. "And hey," he added, "make sure the guys in the press room don't hear about this."

David Torino picked up the slip of paper and began to read. And unlike the thumbsucker from the Chief of Detectives, it quickly got his full attention.

ANTONIA had been much too distracted by Desi's brutal death to give off much artificial charm at the reception. So after one glass of domestic and deflecting the forward passes of a city bureaucrat and a banker, she made up an alibi about Guy having an ear infection, gave her unhappy date a peck and made a hasty exit from the Tavern on the Green.

TALONS

At home in her penthouse apartment on lower Fifth Avenue, a legacy from Mr. Ice, who had died six years earlier, she looked in on her sleeping son Guy, patted the paw of Nanook and noted Mary, the *au pair* girl, snoring gently in front of a rerun of "The Odd Couple" in the den. All's well on the home front, at least, she thought.

She went to the study and tried to work on her monograph on ospreys but found she couldn't concentrate on the evolution of the species' reversible outer toe at this hour and in her present frame of mind. So she went to the kitchen, fixed herself a spiced rum toddy, put on a Peruvian wool sweater and went to sit out on the terrace that wrapped around the apartment. She liked cold weather, found it bracing, conducive to clear or clearer thinking. She looked out south past Washington Square at the man-made pinnacles and precipices of downtown Manhattan. As an ornithologist she appreciated living in a high-rise with a bird's-eye view of the city and its surprising avian life. For hours she would watch the ubiquitous pigeons fluttering from cornice to ledge. Her eyes would trace the swoop of sea gulls on the journey from the Narrows to Long Island Sound. Wrens, sparrows, jays, even hawks and peregrines nested in concrete turrets and roosted on television antennae and satellite dishes.

Birds. Eight-thousand-six-hundred-and-fifty species in the world and who knew how many billions of individuals. Evolved from the reptilian ancestor archaeopteryx, birds had become constant neighbors, benefactors and sometimes rivals. Without them, though, she thought, the planet would be overrun by insects, choked by weeds. And, besides, they were just so damn beautiful, most of them, anyway, and their melodies had no rivals.

Nanook, license and collar jangling, padded over and curled up next to her. A sudden wind swayed the potted pines and Antonia shivered. Nanook, warm as toast in his white double coat, didn't stir. He regarded her with his almond-shaped Asiatic eyes. His ears elongated at the squawk that suddenly came from the climate-controlled greenhouse on the southeast side of the terrace, where Antonia kept her collection of parrots, including cockatoos, macaws, and lovebirds.

She thought about Joe and how annoyed he had been when she took a powder from the reception tonight. She guessed she would have to find a way to make it up to him. While not exactly lovebirds, she and Joe were pretty well-suited to each other, on a superficial level. They enjoyed each other's bodies and quick minds. They liked each other, most of the time. Antonia especially appreciated Joe's sexual fidelity to her, not a small matter when one considered how many women were always throwing themselves at him. It was also an important point in light of her marital history, a welcome change from her passionate girlhood crush on Dr. Malcolm Dunning. Intelligent and astute she was in most areas, but she had walked right into the oldest psychic snare of them all—married the classic distant father figure. She had met him at Cornell, where he taught an elective she took on the nervous system of vertebrates. He had been a popular lecturer, prematurely gray and quick-witted. She fell a ton. But it turned out the expert on the neurology of vertebrates lacked a spine himself, although he certainly had a nervous system. He was obsessively jealous and inclined to squalls of violence. She had given him no cause to be jealous, had been altogether faithful—unlike him. He couldn't resist playing the sexual butterfly, flitting from coed to chorus girl, barfly to bimbo patient. Worst of all was his streak of brutishness. The first time he hit her, she packed up, nestled Guy in the baby pack and moved out, cutting her losses.

That was two years ago when the curtain fell on five years of play-acting at a happy marriage. Not for an instant since had she regretted leaving. Just because she had been snow-blinded by his charm didn't mean she had to be a masochist as well as a dimwit. Still, she never regretted the marriage, because it had, after all, produced the beautiful son who now slept in his room twenty feet away. His invertebrate father avoided the boy, but she did her best to take up the slack. With luck he would survive the trauma of having had a distant father. After all, she had. Or had she? Yes, dammit, she had! Well, more or less...

Feeling sort of blue, she sat there quietly, scratching the husky's head, and looked at the blue-black winter sky studded with stars.

Abruptly she thought about the murdered panda. What an odd and baffling thing. Scary, somehow. She couldn't get it out of her mind. She looked at Nanook and saw in his pointy ears and triangular muzzle a striking resemblance to the panda. Of course, they were related. All mammals were, all living things were connected—

Her child crying brought her out of her reverie, and she was grateful for it. She got up to see what was wrong.

DAVID Torino woke up at daybreak to the cooing of pigeons on his bedroom window sill. A fresh-air nut, even in winter he slept with the window cracked open at the bottom. He hurled a pillow in the direction of the birds, clasped his kneecaps and swung himself out of bed.

He stretched long limbs, scratched his butt through pin-striped boxer shorts and went into the kitchen, where he put on the tea kettle and halved an orange. When his eyes had adjusted he checked the clock over the stove. It was seven-ten on the northern hemisphere that he now occupied, reluctantly, still under the spell of the Southern Cross.

He looked out the window at the raw misty day that dawned over South Street where he lived not for the alleged chic quality of its proximity to the old waterfront but because it was close to police headquarters, where he worked, and to his mother's apartment in Knickerbocker Village.

He drank sweetened tea and frowned at the day ahead. This panda investigation. He loathed taking on a case that political hacks like the Parks Commissioner had a special interest in, hated the notion of being monitored from above. Fascinating, the case also was kind of unsavory, not to say difficult and weirdly puzzling. The lab tests might be back today; he decided to stop in at headquarters to check before heading uptown to the zoo to interview witnesses. All that should distract him some from the afterglow of Argentina.

Torino's restored one-bedroom apartment, in a low-ceilinged eighteenth-century building, faced southeast overlooking the river, the beauty of the Brooklyn Bridge and the towers of Brooklyn beyond. But its dominant feature—one that the real estate agents soft-pedaled if they mentioned it at all—was the constant rumble and toot of traffic on the East River Drive directly outside the window. What a contrast to the breathless silences of aviation. In an unfocused way he had been looking around for a new place.

As he got dressed he pondered again the question so often asked by his mother and sisters—why hadn't he ever married? Well, he had nothing against marriage. As the youngest in a household of three women who had doted on him, he grew up very fond of womankind. Marriage would be nice, he thought. It just hadn't happened. Not yet...David Torino had the kind of emotional life that stirred like a glacier. For long periods he would drift along at a ponderous, imperceptible pace while beneath the icy exterior some erosive agent was at work. Then, somehow, sparked by some mysterious confluence of events, the sheets of ice surrounding his personality would break off and tumble into the waters. He was moving toward that now, he sensed it.

Torino put in contact lenses, holstered his service revolver, and as usual walked to Headquarters. The cold stung his face as he walked up Pearl Street under the bridge viaduct. As an adult he lived in the same polyglot neighborhood between the Brooklyn and Manhattan bridges that he'd grown up in. In those days there were no gourmet restaurants, fancy shops and seaport museums, just the aroma of the Fulton Fish Market and the exhaust fumes from the bridge traffic and the trucks that rattled over the cobblestones delivering the now defunct *Journal-American* from the Hearst building on South Street. But it was as good a place as any to play stickball, bathe in fire hydrants, experience puppy love and perform the other rites of passage to manhood. Better than some neighborhoods he could mention. The family had not been poor—his father, who died in his prime, had been a small wine merchant. They had a modest apartment in the housing project where his mother still lived, with a river view and a small terrace in an age before such amenities in Manhattan became exclusive to the rich. His father's death from pleurisy had come as a hard blow, but his mother and older sisters—Rose and Juliet— had buffered the impact. At fifteen he became the "man of the house," and as such was treated like a prince. A hard act for any woman to follow.

On his desk at Police Plaza lay the results of the panda lab tests. He paused before reading it, still marveling that he had been assigned to investigate the death of a zoo animal, for God's sake. The boss typecast him as some kind of naturalist just because he backpacked on vacations, kept an angora cat and grew an herb garden in the windowbox. Still, it was better than routine drug investigations.

He began reading the folder. Forensics showed nothing useful in the way of physical evidence. No discernible hair follicles or traces of skin or cuticle left behind by the "perp." The animal's breast had been torn open, its heart and lungs ripped out by some kind of sharp "scooplike" implement. "Weapon unknown," Torino scribbled in his notebook.

He continued to read the mumbo-jumbo in the report until on the last page he came across a startling and puzzling entry: an autopsy showed that the animal had died of suffocation.

Six

ANTONIA MADE A point of getting up early enough to eat breakfast with her son before leaving for work. She didn't want to wake up one day to a breakfast of rue in an empty nest. Besides any sense of duty, she *enjoyed* such moments with her son.

They ate in an alcove off the kitchen, surrounded on three sides by windows overlooking the terrace and the bleak sky. Between mouthfuls of cereal Guy sniffled and made funny sounds in his chest.

Antonia glanced at Mary, the *au pair*, the Irish immigrant girl who had lived with them almost since the divorce. "He's coming down with something."

Mary nodded. "The flu's been going around."

"Keep him home from nursery school. I'll phone Dr. Goodman and have him call in a prescription to the pharmacy...You can take the night off, go to the movies or something. Okay?"

"Okay." Actually she preferred the new reggae club that had opened on Bond Street.

Antonia glanced at her daybook. In the morning she was scheduled to lecture at the Graduate Center on the Mystery of Bird Migration, then lunch with a colleague to discuss a joint-grant proposal followed by tennis with Rachel Tauber in midtown, an afternoon meeting at the zoo and a quick drink with Joe at One Fifth.

She got up from the table, gathered the boy in her arms and kissed him squarely on the sticky mouth. Her heart turned to mush. Why didn't she just chuck the schedule and stay home today? There it was, the old tug-of-war. She turned to Mary. "Don't let him go outside, not even on the terrace. I'll have the pharmacy deliver. And don't let him watch too much TV, ok?"

Mary nodded and frowned. "I've seen 'The Little Mermaid' so many times I'm waterlogged."

Antonia laughed, blew Guy a kiss and left the apartment.

In the darkened lecture hall Antonia showed slides of migrating arctic terns and described their habits to those students who hadn't dozed off the moment the lights were dimmed. "The arctic tern," she said without benefit of notes, "is a gypsy among feathered bipeds, making a round trip between breeding seasons of some twenty-two thousand miles from the Arctic to the Antarctic and back again. This bird gets no bonuses for being a frequent flier either."

Scattered chuckles from the students still awake.

"Other species such as the American grosbeak, while not exactly stay-at-homes, would rather wander than migrate according to a fixed pattern, apparently impelled not so much by breeding instincts as by the search for food. Of course most of our theories on bird migration are speculative." She depressed the lever that switched slides and a flock of white whooping cranes appeared onscreen.

Antonia pushed ahead, on cruise-control. Her mind was only partly occupied by the familiar saga of bird migration. It was more absorbed by an idea that had often troubled her. The theme of her talk was "mystery." She knew, like the sages of ancient Greece, that each "scientific" truth unearthed contained the larvae of a new enigma. The process was infinite. How little we know, she once again thought as she went on with an air of authority in front of this sophomoric assemblage in the lecture hall. More specifically, how little *she*, the expert, really knew about birds. The next slide depicted a Great Horned Owl flying at a cottontail, talons poised for the kill. Antonia had seen the photograph many times before. Now, for some reason, it made her uneasy.

After class she usually hung around for a few minutes to allow students to ask questions or, more often than not, to clear up some administrative stuff about credits, assignments, exams, grades. Today, however, she gathered up the material, crammed it into her briefcase and made a beeline for Forty-second Street, where she hailed a taxi. The lunch to discuss the grant proposal was eaten at a West Side sushi bar that produced little more than heartburn. She lost the tennis match, two sets to love.

She arrived at the Arsenal in a black mood.

MEANWHILE Lieutenant Torino had had a more productive morning and afternoon interviewing staff members and poking around the zoo, sharpening his intuition, getting a feel for the place and people.

In the zoo gallery filled with wildlife sculptures he interviewed Curator Al Marburg, whom he quickly tagged as a horse's ass. He asked Marburg about the possibility that the panda had been killed by members of a Dominican or Haitian cult who were known to use the vital organs of animals in religious ceremonies.

"Of course, that's a distinct possibility," said the rotund mammal expert, smelling of some sort of spiced soap, caressing the varnished wood carving of a whale fashioned by Aleutian Islanders. "But I have another notion."

"I'd be most happy to hear it, Mr. Marburg."

"I think it was Koreans," he said, smiling at the apparent ingenuity of his speculation.

"Koreans?"

"Yes. The city is flooded with them. And they're well-known for violating federal and state laws regarding traffic in animal parts."

"I didn't know that."

"Oh, yes. Koreans are single-handedly responsible for the precarious state of the brown bear. Did you know that, lieutenant?"

"No, I'm not too up on the subject."

The detective took a notebook and pencil from his pocket as Marburg went on: "You see, they buy and sell the animal's gall bladder for hundreds, thousands of dollars. They believe that the organ has miraculous curative powers."

"Does it?"

Marburg had moved on to inspect another recently acquired piece, a gold giraffe from Kenya. "Most certainly not," he said, peering at the sculpture. "Beautiful, eh?"

Torino dropped the art appreciation. "Do you know if they have the same ideas about the organs of a panda?"

"It wouldn't surprise me. The *wah* is an Asian creature, you know. Although I don't believe it ever ranged as far east as Korea."

49

Torino scribbled some notes and followed Marburg to a small office off the gallery, where Marburg offered a cigar. Torino declined as Marburg lit up.

Torino waved at the smoke. "The lab tests showed something strange," he said. "The autopsy indicates that the animal didn't die from the wounds but from suffocation."

Marburg took the cigar out of his mouth. "That *is* extraordinary." He reflected a moment. "I really don't know what to make of it."

"Would a man be able to suffocate the animal fairly easily?"

Marburg shrugged. "A very strong man, perhaps. The *wah* has very sturdy transverse condyles and a robust skull."

"Would you mind translating that?"

"He has good bite pressure and powerful chewing muscles. What baffles me is how they trapped him. He's a slippery creature, can scamper up a tree quick as a flash."

"But there are no tall trees in his habitat here."

"True. Still, it would be like getting the devil by the tail."

Torino paused. "Why did you say 'they'?"

"Seems more likely that at least two persons did this. Working together."

"But why suffocate the animal before taking out the organs?"

Marburg rubbed his pink chin. "Beats me."

Torino tried to choose his next words carefully. "I suppose this incident represents a considerable loss to the zoo."

Marburg peered at the cigar butt. "It's a loss to everyone. The red panda's range is shrinking all the time. It's an endangered species. There are a few hundred in zoos and animal reserves around the world. They're elusive creatures and nobody really knows how many survive in the wild. It's also, of course, a loss to the taxpayers of New York. This animal was worth thousands of dollars. We'll also have to find another mate for Lucy. *Wahs* don't grow on trees, you know." He said it with a straight face. "They *are* arboreal animals, you see."

"Sure," said Torino, suppressing a smile. "Do you figure this matter reflects on you as General Curator?"

"Me? Well, it's not exactly a feather in my cap. We'll have to find a way to protect Lucy from the same fate. The panda enclosure is zoogeographic, as we say. Designed with minimum fencing and logs, stumps, rocks and streams to resemble as much as possible the forest habitat. But it is not designed to keep intruders out. Who could have imagined that somebody would want to kill such a creature? It's astounding."

"Have you considered the possibility that some rival for funding, some competitor in the Parks Department or Zoological Society, had something to do with this?"

"Far-fetched," he muttered, although his eyes turned wary. "I'll give the matter some thought." A beat. "Of course, one makes certain enemies of jealous inferiors in one's career. But I sincerely doubt..."

Torino nodded. "I'm inclined to agree, but I have to look at all the possibilities."

"Certainly," said Marburg, glancing at his wristwatch.

Torino took the hint. "I know you must be busy, thanks for your help."

"Yes, indeed," said Marburg, limply accepting the detective's hand.

"I'll find my way out," said Torino.

Marburg wagged the cigar. "Don't forget the Korean angle," he said in a tone reserved for lower primates. "I'd bet a month's salary on it."

As he got to the front door of the zoo gallery, thinking about what an officious ass the curator was, Torino nearly collided with a terrific-looking young woman who had just stepped down from a dado.

"Excuse me," Antonia Meadows said, brushing past him.

He watched her walk into the gallery. And watched, and watched.

LIEUTENANT Torino decided to take a last look at the crime scene before night fell. He walked the wooden path to the Temperate Zone, nodded to the uniformed police officer posted by the enclosure, hopped over the low railing and began poking around.

Lucy, the victim's mate, had been temporarily removed to another place for examination by an animal psychologist, he was told. Psychologist, yet. He moved among the pines and shrubs, peered into a hollow log, crunching dry leaves underfoot. He squatted on the ground, removed his contact lenses and put on powerful prescription glasses. He was just about to give up when he thought he spotted something about six paces away lying near a deeply pitted boulder by the stream. He walked over and stooped to pick up the object.

It was a feather, its auburn color deepened by the ebbing light of the sun. Torino had never seen one like it before. Few had.

Seven

THE SAME RED sun that gilded the feather, evolutionary off-shoot of a reptile's scale, stained the surface of the Atlantic Ocean as viewed from Breezy Point at dusk where fifteen-year-old Jennifer Lichtenberg searched for Fritz, her miniature schnauzer.

Her voice echoed over the sand drifts. "Fritzie! Here, Fritz."

She sounded more annoyed than alarmed. He was always doing this, scampering off the leash on his nightly walks, grubbing in the marshes after chipmunks and mice. She couldn't get too angry. But it was very hard to put up with this in the winter. And her stomach growled for dinner. So she was in a bad mood as she searched the fringes of the beach.

Of course she never stayed pissed at him for too long. One look at that mutton-chopped burgomeister face and those liquid eyes and her heart melted. "Here, Fritzie."

She brushed back her autumn-leaf yellow hair and scanned the horizon. She took a deep breath, looking first toward the inlet, then toward Rockaway Point Boulevard where the street lamps had just blinkered on. She hoped she wouldn't have to search in the reeds. She wasn't wearing boots.

Slowly, tentatively she walked in the direction of the jetty, still calling and whistling, squinting into the velvet dusk. She turtled into the hood of her loden coat. It was dark and the area was deserted. Fritz was nowhere to be seen. Muttering, she looked west from land's end, then east at the winking lights of traffic on the Marine Parkway Bridge. Where could he be? Could he have chased something into the water and drowned? Her teeth chattered in the cold.

Suddenly she heard a loud sound coming from the water's edge on the north side of the roadway. It was an odd sound, like the rustling of dry branches. She turned toward it. She thought she saw a large dark figure gliding low over Rockaway Inlet in the general direction of Coney Island. For a moment she thought it was a huge bat of some sort. Then it vanished into the thickening night.

She turned and hurried toward the family bungalow on Oceanside Street. She hoped that her father, a city firefighter, would have awakened from his nap and would help her look for Fritz in the car. By the time she got to the house she was breathless, and her cheeks were wet with tears.

Scott Lichtenberg was drinking coffee in the kitchen at the rear of the house. Drowsy-eyed. Cranky. He looked older than his forty-one years. He had a gray pallor, prematurely gray hair and slate-gray eyes, which he lifted at his daughter's entrance, prepared to scold her because his wife, who worked as a secretary for a real-estate broker, didn't get home until after six and Jennifer was responsible for putting dinner on the table. When he saw her tears and the look on her face, his expression quickly softened.

"What's the matter, kiddo?"

She told him.

On the way out the front door they passed the television set, on top of which in a gilt frame was a photo of Fritz.

Jennifer and her father drove up and down the peninsula from Jacob Riis Park to the Coast Guard station to Fort Tilden to Rockaway Point. Using a high-beam flashlight, they searched woods, marshes, streets and beaches. Scott Lichtenberg often stuck two fingers into his mouth to produce a high-decibel whistle.

At last they found the dog's body on some rocks near the jetty—his exposed guts were lapped by gentle little waves.

"IF I were still a news hound," said Joe Bannister, sipping designer water with a bobbing wedge of lime, "I'd be on this story in a shot."

"If you were still a news hound," Antonia said, "I wouldn't be telling you about it. Mum's the word. I mean it."

They sat at a marble-topped café table near the end of the bar. A plate of grapes, pâté and cheese was in front of them. Joe Bannister's rather large head, thatched with a mane of sandy hair, wagged with disapproval. "What a waste," he said, "killing a rare beautiful animal like that."

Antonia nodded.

"I wonder how many tax dollars the killer has lost for us—"

"Come on, Joe, who cares about tax dollars? Think about the animal's progeny. That's the real tragedy."

"Don't put down tax dollars, honey. They pay both your salaries." He meant what she earned from both the Parks Department and the City University jobs. "Anyway, you know I'm just as committed to environmental protection as the next guy. Remember, I was the one who persuaded His Honor to crack down on Con Ed's dirty smokestacks.

And not just for political reasons." She didn't want an argument, was distracted by concern about Guy.

"We're really on the same side," he went on. "You just favor the animals over us poor humans."

"Joe," she said, rising to the bait, "do you realize how other life forms sustain each other while mankind mostly destroys? Do you know that some acacias grow hollow thorns to lodge ants? How birds trail army ants to steal their prey while moths follow the whole procession to feed on the bird excrement?"

"Romantic stuff, no question."

She ignored it. "Nature has this symmetry that we throw out of kilter."

"Animals destroy, don't they? They prey on each other. They defoliate like crazy. Ever hear of locusts? Sharks?"

"But animal behavior patterns—excluding man and his interventions, of course—keep nature in harmony. Birds keep the insect population in check. Insects keep the earth from being strangled with vegetation..."

He smiled and refilled her wine glass as she went on. He actually loved the way she would lecture at the drop of a hat. It didn't bother him at all that she was his intellectual superior. He even sort of liked the idea. It took the pressure off.

"Sadly," she was saying, "we're the real predators, we're the only species that hunts and fishes for sport."

"What about the man-eaters? Crocodiles? Sharks? Tigers?"

"The stories about them are exaggerated. The Bengal tiger eats deer and fowl and cattle. The man-eater is an animal past his prime whose teeth are worn-down."

Joe smiled. "So he sets up camp near some thatched-roof village and has wogs à la carte."

She shook her head. "They don't kill without reason, they

don't kill for sport. *And* they don't kill to prove their superiority—or their manhood."

"Well, they kill just as dead," he said. "Hey, don't take it too seriously," he said, and realized immediately he'd said the wrong thing.

"We're talking about what I do," she said tightly.

"I mean, don't take our arguing about it too seriously." He reached across the table and covered her hands with his. "You're right, of course. I gladly bow to your superior knowledge. Also to your superior beautiful dimples. And your gorgeous ass."

"Now you're talking. Nice recovery."

They leaned across the table and kissed. She picked up her purse. "Got to run."

"So early?"

"Mary's waiting for me, and I promised Guy I'd spend the evening with him."

"Don't forget the screening tomorrow night."

"I won't." She paused, took in the flock of young females preening their plumages at the bar. Talk about predators, she thought. "Behave yourself," she told him, wagging a red-nailed forefinger.

"I'm saving myself for marriage," he said. "Speaking of which ... "

She had already turned and left the bar.

THE next morning Antonia found a telephone message on her desk from a Lieutenant David Torino. She frowned at the memo slip. What did a detective of the Major Case Squad want to talk to her about? The panda? But mammals were Marburg's territory. She scanned her daybook, looking for a spot to squeeze in the policeman. Maybe she could postpone seeing him until tomorrow or the next day. Maybe she could sidestep seeing him at all. She picked up the phone and reached Marburg.

"Do you happen to know why a Detective Torino wants to talk to me?"

Marburg, cradling the telephone receiver between his shoulder and jaw, was peeling an orange. "I'm not sure. He asked me if he could speak to my bird specialist. I didn't ask him why. I'm sure he has good reason, although I wasn't very impressed with him when we met."

"What could an ornithologist possibly tell him about the killing of a red panda?" she said.

Marburg popped a section of orange into his round mouth, an organ that mirrored the general shape of the rest of him. "My dear, you must cooperate with this investigation in any way you can. Given the current budget crunch both here and in Albany, I'm afraid that such an incident might encourage politicians to tighten the purse strings on us. Especially if it goes unsolved. It makes us look very bad. Between you and me, I've heard rumors about a big cut in funding from the Natural Heritage Trust. Let's not give them ammunition, eh?"

Antonia sighed, agreed to call the detective and hung up.

THE odor of African pygmy goats, sheep and rabbits reached David Torino's nostrils as he arrived on Fifth Avenue at the outskirts of the park and zoo. Since he was a bit early for his appointment with the ornithologist, Antonia Meadows, he decided to poke his nose around a little.

The afternoon sun blazed in a cloudless sky, making the day unseasonably warm. He walked around the Arsenal past the Heckscher Zoo School and Zoo Theater, which was closed, and stopped to admire the Delacorte Clock with its bronze animals—penguin, goat, hippo, bear and kangaroo—that revolved, cavorted and played musical instruments whenever the gong struck. He thought it a lovely, whimsical sculpture. He visited the sea-lion pool in the Central Garden, surrounded by eight stone eagles, sat on a bench and unwrapped a stick of chewing gum. This Meadows woman, he reflected, had been pretty hostile on the phone and he didn't look forward to interviewing her. He pictured her as middle-aged, with bifocals, salt-and-pepper hair in a bun and a pinched, arid face. He watched the sea lions for a while before getting up and nosing around some more.

In the Polar Circle he became mesmerized by the uncanny eyes and movements of a snow owl perched over a make-shift waterfall, swiveling its head like a mechanical toy.

He walked to a section of the park just west of the zoo near the Temperate Zone and right off the East Drive roadway. Outside the fence that surrounded the zoo he found the entrance to a stone tunnel under the viaduct. Squinting in the darkness, his feet trampling dry leaves, he walked inside.

"Who's that?" came a gritty voice from the shadows.

Torino patted the service revolver under his Burberry trench coat. "You tell me, pal." He moved toward the voice in the shadows. A figure sprawled on the ground began to take form.

The stranger had not mistaken the tone. "I ain't bothering nobody, just lee' me alone."

Torino squatted on his haunches. Unlike many New Yorkers, he had an automatic sympathy for the homeless who sought some warmth in the winter in the nooks and crannies of the city.

The face he focused on now looked frightened. The man lay on a dismantled brown cardboard refrigerator carton, a nubby blue polyester blanket pulled up to his stubby neck.

"How you doing?" Torino said. "What's your name?"

The man paused before answering, "Casey."

"How long you lived here, Casey?"

"It's pretty warm in here, you ain't gonna kick me out, are yuh? I don't wanna go to no raggedy-ass shelter."

Torino shook his head. "How long you lived here?"

"Since about Christmas. Been in the street eighteen months now. I got relatives in the Bronx. I don't rip nobody off, I keep my nose clean."

"Sure, Casey." Torino paused to choose his words. "You like living near the zoo?"

"Sure enough." Casey jerked his head to indicate the world outside. "Better than living in some of them people zoos I've seen the inside of."

Torino reached into his pocket. "Want a stick of chewing gum?"

"Rather have a cig."

"Sorry . . . Casey, were you around here this past weekend?"

"Yeah." He looked wary. "I didn't do nothing, though."

Torino pointed toward the mouth of the tunnel, bathed in daylight, and beyond at the fence that enclosed the panda exhibit. "Did you hear about the animal that was killed? The red panda?"

"Look here, I don't know nothing about it. I don't go around killing no animals, two-legs or four. You gotta believe that."

"I do, I just want to know if you heard or saw anything strange around the panda enclosure Saturday or Sunday. Maybe at night."

Casey shook his head.

"Take a minute to think about it. Try to think hard. It's important. Something that sticks out in your mind, broke your routine, maybe."

Casey scratched his head. "Sure wish I had me a cigarette. Makes my mind clearer."

Torino reached into his pocket and handed over a five-dollar bill from his billfold. "Here, get something to eat too."

"God bless you," Casey said, taking the money. "What kind of animal did you say got killed?"

"A red panda."

"Red? I thought pandas was black and white. Thought that there animal was a coon or a fox or something."

"It was a red panda."

Casey rubbed his feet that were wrapped in rags. "Let's see, Sunday just before dark I did hear a commotion from over there. I remember I built me a fire and was cooking bananas. You ever eat cooked bananas? They're good."

"Matter of fact, I have."

"My mama used to cook bananas."

"What kind of commotion?"

Casey reflected for a moment. "Animal noises, I guess."

Torino sat down on the cardboard and took out his notebook and pen. "Could you describe them, Casey?"

Casey peered at Torino. "You a cop or a reporter or what?"

"I'm a detective."

"Well, first there was like a whistle. *Whee, wheet.* I figured that was the coon, I mean, the panda. It sounded kinda it was in trouble, maybe. You know?"

"Yes. Good. Go on, Casey."

"Heard a lot of different sounds. A *quack*, then a *whuff*. Then I heard some like grunts and scuffling around, like the panda was maybe struggling with something."

Torino scribbled notes. "Did you see anything? Did you go over there?"

Casey shook his head. "Learned a long time ago not to stick my snout where it don't belong."

"But you must have at least looked over from here at the place the sounds were coming from. Do you remember seeing anything unusual?"

Casey hunched his shoulders. "It was getting dark."

Torino stood up. "Okay, then." Another thought occurred. "Did you maybe hear anyone talking, or whispering? Did you hear the sound of a car?"

"No, sir."

Torino stuffed the notebook back into the pocket of his coat and rubbed his fingers to stimulate circulation. "Thanks for your help," he said as he flashed a small penlight at his wristwatch, which told him he had just two minutes before the appointment with the ornithologist. "Got to go."

Casey seemed reluctant to lose Torino's company. "Heard something else too," he suddenly added. "Don't know if it was connected—"

"What was that, Casey?"

"Bells."

"Bells?"

"Yeah, sort of like on an ice-cream truck. Except I know it couldn't be no ice-cream truck in February."

"Maybe the sound came from the merry-go-round?"

Casey shook his head. "It wasn't no music, it was bells. And the sound got louder, quicker when the animal was making those struggling noises. Then I heard it get fainter and fainter till I couldn't hear it no more."

Torino jotted down a note and said, "Thanks again, Casey. I wish to hell I knew what to make of your information."

"Hey, detective, you'll figger it out," he said, and to himself, "and leave me alone."

Torino held up two crossed fingers and moved out of the tunnel.

Eight

LISTING ON SPIKED heels, Fillipina ushered David Torino into Antonia Meadows' office.

As she typed on the keyboard of a computer Ms. Meadows had her back turned to the visitor.

"Lieutenant Torino," Fillipina announced.

Antonia removed her eyeglasses and swiveled around to face him. "Lieutenant?" she said.

Torino's mouth went slack as he shook her outstretched hand.

"Ms. Meadows...thanks for seeing me." In more ways than one, he couldn't help thinking.

"Haven't we met, lieutenant?"

Torino nodded. "We nearly collided at the gallery the other day."

"Yes, right. I remember. Well, sit down." She indicated a small sofa and coffee table near an antlered hat rack.

Torino watched her. Slender but not skinny, tall but not

gangly, sexy but not coquettish, womanly. She had an understated, thoroughbred style. Out of his league?

"Now," she said, briskly, "what can I do for you?"

"It's about the panda," he said.

"I figured. But I'm puzzled. They must have told you that my specialty is *birds*." She stirred her coffee, leaning against the back of the sofa, her face almost brushing the tendrils of a hanging spider plant.

Ridiculous, but it was like he was hypnotized.

"Well?"

"Oh, I know you're an ornithologist." He fumbled in the pocket of his tweed coat. "Here, I wanted to ask you about this." He brought out an object in plastic wrap. "It's a feather," he said the obvious, holding it up.

She held out her hand; he handed it to her. She examined it briefly, then gave it back. "So?"

"I found it in the red panda enclosure," he told her. "Could you tell me what kind of feather it is?"

She looked disbelievingly. "You found *this* at the scene? You consider it a clue?"

"Could be. That's what I'm here to find out. I assume that finding a feather at a zoo isn't an unusual event."

"We have no free-flying birds at the Central Park Zoo," she said.

"I'm sure there are plenty of bird feathers in Central Park," he said.

"Not like this one." The failing light of day coming through the window highlighted the right side of her face, sharpening her features. Which at the moment added to a baffled look.

"Yes, I figured this didn't belong to any pigeon."

"No, indeed. It's the primary of a haggard, a mature bird. Some kind of large hawk. Offhand, I'd say it probably came from a golden eagle."

"An *eagle*?"

"I can't be sure without doing an analysis, maybe a buteo of some kind..."

"You mean there are buzzards and eagles flying around New York City? Where'd it come from, Staten Island?" It was supposed to be a joke.

"No. No large raptors have bred in the wild around here for decades—more than a century. There used to be a lot of them in the Hudson Highlands, though."

"Raptors? What are raptors?"

"Birds of prey, lieutenant."

"What do these raptors prey on?"

"Depends on the species. Other birds, mostly."

"How about red pandas?"

"You're way off base, lieutenant."

"Don't some birds prey on mammals?"

"Yes, the larger slower ones. The soaring hawks. Many of the *stringiformes*."

"Stringi-who?"

"Owls. Sorry, too many lecture halls. But, getting back to your question, the raptors who prey on mammals attack mostly small animals—mice, opossum, hare. They also eat reptiles like lizards and snakes."

Torino jotted a note. "Why did you say, 'mostly' small animals?"

"There are always exceptions. If the bird is hungry enough, big enough, desperate and daring enough. There's much to be learned about their behavior patterns." Antonia looked wary and somewhat put out by the line of questioning. "I really don't like speculating like this. Eagles and other raptors have been persecuted enough without our feeding the flames."

Torino backed off a little. "Sure, I understand. How far away do these large hawks live, in the wild? Just out of curiosity."

"Well, sometimes the golden eagle winters in the mountains of northwestern New Jersey—Raccoon Ridge in the Kittatinny Mountains, Hawk Mountain in Pennsylvania. Not around here, though. The last time a specimen was spotted on Long Island was back in 1950."

He allowed a smile. "Before you were born."

"You, too."

He nodded, grateful for any personal recognition on her part. "Didn't I read somewhere about birds of prey nesting in skyscrapers?"

"Yes, accipiters and peregrines."

"There you go again," he said, smiling, risking.

"Sorry. Bird hawks and falcons. They love insurance buildings, for some odd reason, and they get fat off of pigeons. Some scientific outfits even released them to breed in cities on an experimental basis, to increase their populations. The projects have been very successful."

"What about large hawks in captivity around here?"

"There's a raptor preserve nearby in New Jersey. Eagles, buzzards, owls. But the birds are caged."

"Might one have escaped?"

"Not without my hearing about it. Please, Lieutenant Torino. I really think you're wasting your time pursuing this. And mine."

"Ms. Meadows, I'm a detective, I have to explore all sorts of far-out possibilities. If I'm on the wrong track, please set me straight. That's why I'm here. And I'm sorry if I ruffled your feathers. So to speak."

She let it pass. "I suppose as a scientist I should sympathize with your open-minded methodology."

"And there's the question of the feather." He held it up again.

"Perhaps some native American cult was at work here? The Iroquois considered the golden eagle an invisible spirit, 'the Great War Eagle' of Hiawatha. Their feathers are prized and used in rituals, I believe, although anthropology isn't my field."

"I haven't seen too many Iroquois around New York lately—except maybe in the East Village."

"What happened to the open-minded methodology?"

"Okay, this is New York and *anything's* possible." Add American Indians to the Haitians, Dominicans, and Koreans. He then told her about Marburg's suspicions.

"Well," she said, "that's a lot more plausible than raptors. Eagles are very man-shy and city-shy."

When she excused herself to take a call from the Bronx Zoo Torino got up from the sofa and browsed around the office. On the wall were what he guessed were two original prints by Audubon. On her desk in a plain silver frame was the photograph of a tow-headed little kid. He had noted that she wore no wedding ring. He picked up the photograph.

She hung up the phone and looked up at him.

"Handsome boy," he said.

"Thank you. My son, Guy."

"How old?"

"Three." She paused. "Children, Lieutenant Torino?"

He shook his head. "Never been married." He took the plunge. "Been married long?" he asked.

"I'm divorced."

"Oh." He tried not to look pleased. "Sorry."

"I'm not, I'm engaged to be married again."

"Congratulations."

"Thank you."

"Lucky fellow."

She waved it off.

He was annoyed that he felt jealous.

She looked at him. "May I say something personal?"

"Of course."

"It's hard to believe you're a cop."

"I can show you my shield."

"No, what I meant was, you don't look like a cop, you don't talk like a cop, you don't act like a cop."

"Thanks," he said. After a pause, "I think."

"I meant it as a compliment."

"I wasn't always a cop."

"Oh?"

"I was an altar boy. A philosophy major. A fighter pilot—"

"An unusual curriculum vitae. Apples and oranges."

"So they tell me. I see it as a logical progression." Don't sound defensive, he told himself.

"You'll have to explain it to me sometime."

"Just name the hour and place."

She consulted her wristwatch. "I have a meeting with my directors in twenty minutes." Her smile was official. "Hope I've been of some help, lieutenant."

He shook her hand. "You have. Thanks."

"And I hope you get to the bottom of this ugly business."

"I'll do my best."

She went with him to the door.

"One thing I forgot to mention," he said, snapping his fingers. "Maybe you know what to make of it."

"Yes?"

"The autopsy—it showed that the red panda hadn't died of its wounds but of suffocation. Isn't that strange?"

The sound of the assistant's typing came through the half-open door. As the day darkened electric lights had been turned on in the outer office. "Very strange," Antonia said.

"Any ideas?" he asked.

Her hand still on the doorknob, she said, "No, none at all." She looked at him with a quick smile. "Sorry."

"Will you give it some thought?"

"Certainly. Good-bye, Lieutenant Torino."

SHE was running late. On the taxi ride to the Bronx she
could not focus on the meeting with the zoo directors but
kept turning over in her mind the interview with Lieutenant
David Torino. On many levels it had been an unsettling
experience and she sensed the need to sort out her feelings.
She closed her diary with a clap and gazed out the car window at the deserted athletic fields of Randall's Island at the
junction of the East River and Harlem River, a place made
ghostly by the shroud of evening. The encounter with the
detective had sparked conflicting emotions—confusion, excitement... even fear? She felt a magnetic attraction to the
man. Dammit, she *did*. As the lights of the Triborough
Bridge came into view she tried to think it was based on
his avine appearance—a combination of birds, the ungainly
grace of a flamingo, the regal profile of a hawk, without the
ferocity of a predator but with a core of strength. Oh, come
on, Antonia. This isn't a bird, it's a *man*...

DAYLIGHT had ebbed to a pale blue memory by the time
they hit the Sheridan Expressway in the Bronx, the only
borough of New York City located on the mainland of
America. After checking her wristwatch and politely prod-
ding the driver to make better time, Antonia sank back into
reflection. She hated these late afternoon meetings with the
starched shirts who held the purse-strings. The formal
agenda involved discussing the budget for the new design
of the Polar Circle exhibit, but she was sure that the killing
of the *wah* would figure in the conversation. She would
contribute little or nothing to the subject. As an ornithol-

ogist, she decided, she had nothing helpful to say. Did she?

Reaching the south end of Bronx Park, Antonia thought about what Torino had told her about the animal having been suffocated. The idea that crept in like an intruder, unwanted and outlandish, made her doubt her senses. The feather. Suffocation. She remembered reading somewhere how certain large birds of prey sometimes suffocated their victims. One and one made two. Or did they?

The cab stopped on the leafy edge of Fordham Road. She got out of the car, paid the fare, put on her best authoritative face and banished the implausible notion from her thoughts.

Nine

JOE BANNISTER SAT in a leather armchair and watched Mayor Bill Santiago mouth his popcorn platitudes and flourish charm like a magic baton. As the boyish politician spoke and paced, Bannister marveled, as he often had in the past, that such a man held the tiller of the most important city in the world.

But Santiago had vaulted many seemingly insurmountable barriers to stand where he stood today, lecturing a group of powerful men and women from behind the gleaming hardwood desk of the chief executive of New York City. The obstacles had included the handicap of poverty, the impediment of race and, above all perhaps, the barbed wire of belonging to the wrong party. Bill Santiago was the first Puerto Rican in history, and the first Republican, to occupy City Hall since John V. Lindsay left the office in 1974, more than twenty years earlier. He had made it on cunning, intelligence, a kind of pyrotechnical way with words, a little double-dealing and a lot of dumb luck. It also helped that he had a big-city voting record in Congress and, most of all, that his Democratic opponent had entered the campaign bloodied by a knock-down-drag-out primary battle. Santiago still would have lost the election, Bannister felt, were it not that two weeks before the polling the Democratic candidate's wife was arrested in a drunk-driving accident. Not a mortal blow in itself but enough to teeter him over the brink.

To such an opportune convergence of fortune Joe Bannister owed his job. He and Bill Santiago were old friends, played minor league baseball together in their youth. The congressman and the television anchorman, both luminaries on the urban scene, had kept in touch through the years although they had not been exactly bosom pals. It was Bannister who put out the first feeler about the press secretary job and Santiago liked the idea. This too represented a departure from tradition, since mayoral press aides usually were recruited from the ranks of print journalists, electronic reporters being considered more lightweight and superficial, not really political timber. But Bill Santiago, who broke the mold in many ways himself, did not mind trashing tradition in such matters and relished the notion of bossing around the TV star who had been star pitcher for the Albany Poltroons Triple-A team while he had warmed the pines. Besides, he must have appreciated Bannister's credentials for the job—his cool air of authority before the camera, sharp mind, and effectiveness behind the scenes.

Furthermore, Bannister and Santiago seemed to worship in the same church before the altar of ambition. Still, Bannister thought, he was being rather harsh on himself. Traces of altruism and reformist tendencies sometimes edged into his mentality. He did want to use his talents for something more than reading news off a teleprompter.

Deep down he wanted to make the city a better place to live in, but he didn't like to admit even to himself that higher motives ever entered the picture. He seemed to have a psychological vested interest in his own cynicism. He cultivated an image of himself as a knave behind a handsome façade. And the base metal of Bannister's personality was mixed with the silver of a real affection for Antonia Meadows. She, he reflected as Santiago droned on, brought out not the best in him or the worst in him but at least she brought out *him*, not the mock-up that most people, including himself, saw.

Bill Santiago was riding high in power and popularity, even planning a New York World's Fair celebrating the turn of the century and the dawn of the Third Millennium. Preparations for "Expo New Millennium" were still in the preliminary stages but the Mayor was fired up by the idea. Laying the groundwork for the fair and going through the approval process was expected to take some time; it was slated to begin in three years, in 1999, and last for two years, spanning both centuries and millennia. Santiago saw it as a way to engrave his name in the history books as the impresario of the biggest and best World's Fair ever. Of course it would help matters if he could persuade the Governor and certain power brokers that the exposition would also make money. That too was the subject of the present meeting.

"In conclusion," Santiago said, sitting down and lacing his hands behind his head, "I believe the World's Fair of 1999–2000 could be the biggest such event of its kind since London's Crystal Palace Exhibition of 1851."

Understatement, thought Bannister, was never one of Bill's strong points, but this time he might very well be right. If they all played their cards right.

"Who's our competition?" Santiago said.

Deputy Mayor Helmut Frank consulted notes. "Istanbul,

Trieste, Athens and Punta del Este. The way I see it, Athens is our only real rival."

Santiago looked puzzled. "Where's Punta del Este?" The Latin Mayor looked a little sheepish at his ignorance.

"Uruguay," Frank said. "It's practically a satellite of Buenos Aires, though."

"I see," said Santiago, who didn't.

Richard Breglio, Deputy Mayor for Economic Development, a graph-slide-show-and-pointer type, began to outline ways the exposition might attract tax and tourist dollars to the city. As Breglio droned on Bannister considered the Mayor's personal motives for pushing so hard on what might turn out to be a harebrained idea. He remembered Santiago telling him that his father had worked as a security guard at the United States pavilion of the 1964–1965 New York World's Fair. What was the theme of that one? "Peace Through Understanding," or some such. Santiago was just a kid at the time but the event seemed to have made a lasting impact on him. He liked to talk about how growing up in Queens the Unisphere, the big stainless steel globe built in Flushing Meadow for the fair, inspired him to go for a career in politics to "bring people together." Corny, but maybe he really believed it.

"Okay," said Santiago, after Breglio was done, "let's get back about where to locate it."

Somebody said Coney Island would be a wonderful site, with the parachute jump and all, right on the ocean.

"Coney Island is a war zone," Bannister said. "I say we hold it in Flushing again. The site is ready-made, it would cost very little to spruce it up. It's accessible to lots of transportation. We'll have to work out a few traffic problems but they'll be no sweat. It's right next door to Shea Stadium and the National Tennis Center. Close to the airports. It's ideal." While he didn't mention it outright Bannister also was well aware that the site was in Queens, Santiago's own political turf.

"I agree," said Santiago. "I'm thinking about the parachute jump, though. And the globe. We need some big symbolic structures. Like the Eiffel Tower. That was built for a world's fair, wasn't it?"

"Right," said Bannister. "And the Space Needle in Seattle."

The Mayor turned to Helmut Frank. "You work on that one."

"You got it, Bill."

"What's next?" said Santiago, looking around.

"A prospectus for the Bureau of International Expositions," said Frank's assistant.

Bannister quickly decided that a would-be quarterback needed the ball. "I'll write it, Bill."

"Good, Joe. I'll need a draft by early March."

The rustling of papers, scuffling of chairs and small talk signaled that the meeting was over.

High time, Bannister thought, looking at the wall clock. It was nearly eight P.M., and he had a date with Antonia for the movie screening. He made his way from the Mayor's office in the west wing to the domed rotunda near the cantilevered double staircase, a place where for two centuries major deals had been brokered, huge sums of money extorted or paid in bribes, reputations slandered, political fortunes shattered and built.

Waving to the Mayor, he walked through the metal detector and exited the arched door of City Hall. He stood for a moment under the stone colonnade of the entrance and looked at the flood-lit parking area and City Hall Park, where in colonial days public executions had been held, thinking about the report he had to write on the exposition. A lot rode on it. The exposition notion might be a risky one, but the Mayor was committed to it, and he was committed to the Mayor. And the last thing they needed was news getting out about the zoo's biggest attraction being gutted by some nut case. His driver pulled up and Bannister climbed into the blue Mercury.

Ten

WHEN LIEUTENANT TORINO left the Central Park Zoo after the interview with Antonia Meadows he hopped a city bus heading downtown via Broadway to Headquarters. Although it was around rush hour he managed, miraculously, to find a seat on the west side, closer to the sidewalk where the vehicle made the downtown stops.

As he looked through the bus window at pedestrians criss-crossing Fifth Avenue in the cold he realized he had neglected to mention to Antonia Meadows the homeless man's story about the bells. Well, he probably shouldn't give much weight to the words of a wino who heard bells. Still, experience had taught him that keys could crop up in the most unlikely places. From the least likely people...

As the bus turned east at Fortieth Street Torino saw the great stone lions that adorned the staircase of the main building of the New York Public Library, and was reminded again of the red panda. The more he thought about it the more this bizarre killing bothered him. He considered the explanation that the animal had been destroyed in some kind of barbarous ritual. Whatever, slaughter of a rare animal like the red panda was a damned outrage. In spite of his dislike of Marburg, he thought his theory about a Korean black market for animal organs might not be so farfetched. He'd look up an old acquaintance and contact, the editor of the Korean *Daily Journal* on the west side of Manhattan. Dr. John Chang Kim. He'd give him a ring when he got to Headquarters.

As the bus stopped for a traffic light at Canal Street Torino got off and walked the rest of the way to Headquarters. Passing the Clocktower Building on Leonard Street, he noticed for the first time the stone eagles perched on the balustrade under the clock.

"WE fit well, don't we, Antonia?" She and Joe had just finished making love in front of her fireplace.

"Meaning?"

"We dovetail. We're a match."

"Yes," she said in a distant tone. "We fit well."

The fire now crackled loudly.

"You never said how you liked the movie," he said.

"It was okay, I guess, but special effects aren't my thing. One explosion after another. What's the point?"

"The kids eat it up," said Bannister, "and they buy the tickets. Anyhow, shooting the film in New York earned the city some nice tax dollars."

"How many?"

"Who knows? A cop's salary for a few years."

His comment reminded Antonia of Torino and his speculations about the killing of the red panda. She lay on her stomach, propping her chin in her hand. "I met the detective who's working on the panda case."

"Oh?" Bannister said, "some kind of animal expert?"

"I don't think so. Interesting guy, really. Ex-fighter pilot. Sort of unusual for a cop."

"What's his name? Maybe I know him."

"Torino."

Bannister shook his head.

"I think he said he was from the Major Case Squad or something like that."

"They're a pretty elite group."

Antonia pushed back ringlets of hair. "He seemed nice..."

Bannister looked at her.

"But I'm not so sure about his competence. He had some pretty far-out theories about the killing."

"That so? Like what?"

She shook her head in exasperation. "He found a feather in the panda enclosure. It's the primary of a large hawk..."

"So?"

"So he asked me questions about whether the animal might have been killed by some large bird of prey. Like an eagle—"

"Christ! Could it have?"

"Of course not. There are no predators like that in the city."

"I hope not! But what about the feather?"

She shrugged. "Who knows? It could have come from an ornamental headdress. Or maybe it was one of those old-fashioned writing quills. Eagle feathers were used for that."

"Not likely."

"Well, more likely than the idea of a wild bird of prey. Hey, how about it blew off the feather duster of a maid in a Fifth Avenue high-rise."

"Now who's being far-out?" He paused. "Do eagles prey

on big animals? I thought they ate birds and mice and that sort of thing."

"Oh, I suppose it's possible in a *very* extreme case for, say, a large golden eagle to attack and kill an animal the size of the red panda...there's a Philippine eagle that kills and eats monkeys. Some Chinese eagles have been reported to kill foxes. As far as raptors go, the Great Horned Owl is a pretty mean customer...But, in New York City, I'd say we've got enough to worry about with all the human raptors roaming the streets." Her voice strained to sound lightly ironic, but her face betrayed some real concern.

Bannister, putting on his coat, said, "That's all we need, a wild eagle in this city." He hesitated before adding, "Wouldn't *that* be a downer for the exposition!" He had told Antonia about the project earlier in the evening.

"I wouldn't lose any sleep over it, Joe." But she didn't mention the panda's suffocation. Instead, she sat for a moment, then said, "Ever heard of the Neil Eagle legend, Joe?"

"Can't say that I have."

"It's a folktale about an old man in Lapland. He was called Neil Eagle because he was carried off as a baby by a bird of prey—a sea eagle or golden eagle. It's this kind of hogwash and superstitious legend that still has hold of people's minds in parts of Scandinavia, and beyond. Eagles carrying off children and fighting with men."

"Sounds like old-wives'-tale mumbo-jumbo to me," said Bannister. "Sort of like our bogeyman tales to scare the kids into line."

Antonia looked grateful. "Exactly," she said. "Myth, not science."

"Well, gotta get going," he said, and planted a kiss on her mouth.

After he had gone Antonia sat on the old davenport by the snapping fire, absorbed in thought. She sat there for a long time, mildly irked with herself, though she couldn't have said exactly why. Normally she had little talent for idleness or reverie. After a while she got up and went over to the bookcase flanking the fireplace and browsed the shelves until she found a book of poems by Tennyson. Resting her weight on one foot, she riffled the pages for a few seconds, then read:

> He clasps the crag with crooked hands,
> Close to the sun in lonely lands;
> The wrinkled sea beneath him crawls;
> Ring'd with the azure world, he stands,
> He watches from the mountain walls,
> And like a thunderbolt he falls.

She closed the book. In lonely lands, the poet wrote. *Lonely lands.* What could be lonelier for a wild thing than civilization...

Obeying an impulse she would not want to question too closely, she moved quietly into Guy's bedroom, listened to his breathing, pulled the covers closer around him.

SOME ninety-five miles from Greenwich Village, just outside the village of Phoenicia in the heart of the Catskill Forest, Red Bushnell was awakened by the clock radio in his trailer home. He had set the thing for three A.M. and, sure enough, right on time the murmurous voice of a woman paid to stroke insomniacs over the airwaves filled the cold musty interior of the widower's residence.

Bushnell, a carpenter when he could get work, maneuvered his skinny butt into a sitting position and switched on the electric heater, took a swig of rye from the bottle on the bedside table, lit a cigarette and started feeling ready to

81

face full consciousness. At least as ready as he ever got nowadays since Milly died and left this gaping hole in his life.

After a while he went over to the closet and took out his Remington bolt-action thirty-aught-six hunting rifle, put one round in the chamber and four in the clip, then took a flashlight and duct-taped it to the bottom of the barrel. After a second cup of bad joe he would be ready to jack some whitetail deer.

Jacking deer at night was an art at which Red Bushnell used to excel, he thought as he looked over at the fifteen-cubic-foot chest freezer where he would store the venison if he was successful. Lately, he realized, he'd been losing his touch. His eyes weren't what they used to be, and he didn't seem to be able to move as stealthily as he used to. At fifty-five a man started to slow down. He finished the coffee, laced his boots, put on his down coat and flannel hat and went outside.

The night was as black as a bucket of tar. He climbed into the equally black Jeep Cherokee Laredo that he bought in 1991 for more than fifteen grand. He was flush in those days. He wondered how many deer he had tied to the luggage rack in the five years since he had bought the car. On the way back he would use back roads to avoid running into any rangers or state cops but for now he took the highway south past Stony Clove in the direction of Slide Mountain, the highest point in the Catskills. Red Bushnell had few qualms about hunting deer out of season; he did it to put meat on the table. The local cops understood this and rarely messed with the woodchucks who jacked deer. But the state gendarmes and rangers could be pains in the ass. So there was no point taking unnecessary chances, which was why he hunted in the middle of the night. For sure he couldn't afford the $2,000 fine and having his car impounded.

In the foothills he turned off the main road and parked

the jeep in the usual spot under a clump of trees where it wouldn't be found in ten years unless you knew it was there. Snow crunched underfoot as he then made his way deep into the woods. Snow made tracking easy, and soon he found with his flashlight the spoor of what seemed to be a pretty good-sized stag. After a while, when the sixth sense he had about such things told him this was the right spot, he positioned himself behind a big old pine tree at the edge of a clearing and waited, still as a rock.

This was what he loved about stalking prey. His senses were heightened. He was a man alone in the middle of the forest, attuned to every rustle and whisper of nature's creatures. He himself was an integral part of the living, susurrant landscape. Here he was not an interloper. Here he belonged.

You waited until you spotted the eyes, red pinpoints in the velvet night. He'd come all right; deer never strayed very far from the place of their birth, from their habitat. They didn't migrate or anything like that. They were like men of Red Bushnell's ilk: local yokels from birth to burial.

Waiting there, Bushnell lost track of time, merging with the forest and the night, *hearing* the woods, the movements of insects, rodents, reptiles, birds. His thoughts drifted to Mildred, her softnesses combined with her flinty ways and sour humor. Now she too had entered the cycle, feeding the worms who in turn provided food for other creatures of the night. While he jacked deer.

His patience was wearing thin. How long had he been stalking? Dawn was coming. Soon the flashlight would be useless, but visibility would be good with the snow and the sharper contrasts of the half-light. A fairer contest. Although he was out for meat, not sport, the sporting instinct was still strong in him.

As pale light tinctured the rim of the horizon he spotted the eyes glowing in the clearing. He froze, resisting the impulse to square his red cap. The animal couldn't see the cap—his vision was poor and he was color-blind. But the stag had an uncanny sense of hearing and smell.

Now! Bushnell switched on the flashlight.

The deer, ears elongated, froze in the nimbus of light. The rifle cracked once. The deer fell.

Bushnell's body relaxed. As always he felt this surge of kinship with his victim, though he wouldn't have put it that way. Dawn broke, bleaching the clearing where the dead stag lay. He walked out to inspect the animal before going to get the car and his implements. It had been a well-placed shot in the head. He was pretty certain the deer was stone-dead but he wanted to make certain. He also wanted to work fast, just in case some ranger was lurking around, although he doubted it at this hour.

He stood over the immobile carcass—and cocked an ear. What was that? For a moment he thought—imagined—he had heard the sound of a bell? He looked up. Something was soaring low across the field toward him. Surely his eyes played tricks on him. Now it was the man's turn to be petrified.

Eleven

"PRIMITIVE BIRDS WERE fast runners before they were able to fly," lectured Professor Antonia Meadows. "Flight probably evolved from long leaps ... "

David Torino sat unnoticed in the rear of the large hall, wondering how many of the young men in the room had his reaction to Professor Meadows.

Antonia went on with her lecture on "The Mechanics of Bird Flight." "The shape of a bird's body, with the wings inserted high up on the breastplate counterbalanced by the placement of heavier vital organs below, situates the center of gravity below the center of suspension, also facilitating flight ... "

Torino thought about the F-15 that he flew in the Air Force. It had a wonderful design too. So did the professor.

Now Antonia was lecturing on the function of feathers in flight, reminding the detective of the eagle feather he had found in the panda exhibit and his gumshoeing earlier in the day. The visit to Dr. Kim at the Korean *Daily Journal* had pretty much convinced him that Marburg's hunch about organ peddling was a total blind alley. Dr. Kim, whom Torino considered a highly credible source and a scrupulously honest person, conceded that some of his compatriots dealt in contraband gall bladders, but he assured the detective that Koreans had no tradition of prizing the hearts and lungs of animals; furthermore, he and most of his countrymen had never heard of the *wah*, which, he understood from newspaper accounts, ranged no farther east than Sichuan in central China, hundreds of miles from Korea.

From the newspaper office Torino had headed downtown to Greenwich Village to visit the showroom of a feather trader on Twelfth Street. Sophia Gelb, owner of the wholesale feather outlet called The Proud Peacock, peered at the quill that Torino held in his hand. "Golden eagle," she said in a flash. "I know my feathers." On the shelves behind her was a dazzling array of boas and hatbands, marching-band plumes and feather-trimmed geegaws. She shook her head. "We don't use them. Let's see, we got turkey feathers and maribou feathers. Ostrich feathers and, of course, peacock feathers. But no eagle feathers."

"Are eagle feathers used for anything at all?"

"Indian bonnets," she said. "Hatbands, maybe. They ain't fancy enough for most decorative uses." She primped her brassy titian hair.

"How about dusters or mattresses?"

"Nah. Turkey feathers are best for dusters and goose-down, of course, for mattresses and comforters."

Torino lapsed into a disappointed silence.

"I know one use for eagle feathers," she said into the void.

"What's that?"

"Flying." . . .

"Of course," Antonia was now saying, nearing the end of

the lecture, "birds use their feathers for display as well as for flight..."

Torino caught himself wool-gathering. Was he getting moony over this woman? Could be. Looking at her beautiful hair and porcelain skin, bright clothing and jewelry, Torino reflected that the birds of paradise hardly rivaled Antonia Meadows in dazzling the eye. But, he recalled, the females of the genus were plain and drab. The recent involvement with birds, beasts, feathers and bows now sparked images of heraldry in the cop's mind. He pictured her as a damsel in distress and himself as a knight locked in chivalric struggle with some winged dragon. The hard-bitten cop that composed a part of his personality rebelled at this daydream, but the other side of him rather liked the idea.

Torino approached her after the lecture. "Professor Meadows?"

She looked up in surprise from the briefcase into which she had been jamming notes and books. "Lieutenant Torino! Please call me by my first name."

"And I'm David."

"Okay, what brings you here, David? A scientific interest in birds?"

"Sort of."

She checked her watch. It was three-forty-five. "How did you know I was here?"

"I called your office. I hope you don't mind..."

"Not at all. What can I do for you?"

"I have a few more questions, I'm afraid. Is there someplace...?"

She led him to the cafeteria, where they ordered watery coffee.

"I've been doing a little checking," he said, grimacing at his first sip. "It was an eagle feather, all right."

"Oh...so?"

"Remember you said something about eagles shying away from cities and not being comfortable around people?"

"Yes..."

"Are there exceptions to the rule?"

She traced her cheek with her forefinger. "Well, of course there are exceptions to every rule. I mean, there are no absolutes about this kind of thing."

He waited.

"Under certain circumstances..."

"What circumstances?"

"Well, if, for instance, the eagle had been trained to the lure it then might be accustomed to human beings."

"Trained to the lure?"

"Yes, by a falconer."

"Eagles are used in falconry? Aren't they too big?"

"Yes, smaller birds are more commonly used in hawking, although all raptors in one way or another or at one time or another have been trained for the hunt. Even owls. In medieval Europe the eagle was reserved for the emperor." She smiled at the coffee cup. "Sorry, I thought I was through lecturing for the day."

"Well, it's all very interesting."

"But it's *highly* unlikely that an eagle would winter in New York City and attack an animal in a zoo. Really."

"But not impossible, I gather. What if the bird built a nest in, say, Staten Island? Or on the Palisades across the Hudson in New Jersey?"

"Right, Sherlock."

"Okay," he said, "but—"

"Look, lieutenant...David...Eagles have always been an object of fear, mostly irrational. Roman legionnaires carried them into battle to scare their enemies. But they were carrion birds." She finished her coffee.

He pointed at the cup. "Want another?"

She replied with an eloquent grimace.

"How does the eagle overcome the prey?"

"I don't like talking about this. You realize falconry with eagles is forbidden by federal statute in most cases and tightly regulated when it is permitted."

"So is drug use."

Her mouth tightened. "These birds need our *protection*. The Golden Eagle Act puts the species under federal protection where it belongs. Did you know there used to be bounties paid for eagle's feet by ranchers and farmers?"

"But eagles do prey on mammals..."

"*And* fish."

"Who preys on eagles?"

"People with guns," Antonia said. "And that has to stop."

"Look," said Torino, "I'm a conservationist myself. Let's get that clear. But I've got this job and—"

"I understand," she said quickly.

"Okay, then do you mind if I ask a few more academic questions?"

"Shoot." She didn't smile when she said it.

"Well, the eagle slams into the prey. How does it finish off the animal?"

"It usually binds the spine of the animal, paralyzes it."

"With its teeth?"

"No. With the talons."

Torino held up his own hands and looked at them.

She nodded. "The eagle's black claws are her main weapons. They easily penetrate leather. They can snap a man's arm like a twig. If the animal tries to bite, the eagle might bind its nose and..." She didn't finish, obviously was reluctant to do so.

"And..." he prompted.

"And... suffocate the animal."

He said nothing. He didn't have to.

*   *   *

89

TALONS

At home Torino played back the messages on his telephone answering machine. Among them was a reminder from his sister Juliet that they had a date Saturday to see an exhibit of Byzantine art at the Metropolitan Museum. It would be good to see her again, they'd seen precious little of each other since she and John had moved to Upper Saddle River in New Jersey to give the kids a more serene setting for their childhood than the calicoed streets of New York's Lower East Side.

Torino watched a Knick game on television, listened to a Beatles tape over a second glass of Scotch and then hit the sack. But he tossed and turned. He heard the wind chime on the balcony sound through the window that he had opened just a crack in the bedroom. He thought about Patagonia, saw the herds of guanaco stepping like toe-dancers over the crusty brown earth. But recollections of Argentina did not soothe him now. As he drifted toward the threshold of sleep he began to see these animals not as symbols of a pristine world but as what they in essence were—quarry.

He awoke at daybreak, suddenly aware that he had forgotten again to mention something to Antonia Meadows. As soon as he arrived at Headquarters he phoned her and, though reluctant at first, she agreed to see him at her apartment that evening. She needed to be home with her son, so if he didn't mind...

He didn't.

Twelve

IN HER OWN digs and out of the lecture hall, Antonia Meadows was, Torino thought, a different woman, or at least seemed so. He told himself not to jump to conclusions, reminded himself that it was fairly well-known that she and that pretty boy Joe Bannister from the Mayor's office were an item of some kind, but what the hell, he could hope.

And he hoped even more when she suggested he forget his original request for coffee and join her for a martini, which she prided herself on making extra dry. He looked at her, the swan in her habitat. She was wearing a beige blouse, green paisley vest, and twill trousers. On the wall behind her, illumined by halogen spots, hung a tapestry depicting a medieval hawking party. The living room's formality— the carved marble mantel of the fireplace, the Empire candelabra on the side table—was tempered by an old Wurlitzer jukebox abutting the east wall.

The many sides of Antonia Meadows, he was thinking, when a terrific-looking little boy ran into the room and squeezed her a welcome. She quickly introduced him as her three-year-old son Guy, who detached himself from his mother and squeezed Torino's hand like he meant it.

When the boy had left the room Torino said Guy looked very much like his mother. She said she was glad to hear it but that he actually looked more like his father. She sounded as though she wasn't too thrilled about that and he didn't pursue it.

"You said you forgot to tell me something?"

"What? Oh, yes." Back to reality. "Before I interviewed you the other day I poked around the park and ran into a homeless guy who lives in the tunnel near the panda enclosure. He said something that may or may not have a bearing on this thing. I just thought I'd bounce if off you."

"All right."

"He said that at about the projected time of the killing he heard a lot of animal noises from the direction of the exhibit."

"That's not too surprising."

"He also said that he heard bells."

"Bells?"

"Yes. And after the commotion, the sound of the bells got progressively dimmer until it stopped."

Antonia's mouth was slightly open. Her sea-green eyes glittered.

"It means something to you?"

" 'As the falcon her bells,' " she said in an abstracted tone.

"Huh?"

She turned to him, eyes flinty. "Shakespeare. Listen, David, falconers tie bells to the hawk's leg to help them find the bird and quarry after a strike. Or to locate a bird in training that fails to return to the hack."

Torino kept silent, waited.

"Probably just another coincidence," she said. "It's all so fantastic, even the idea of it. But I suppose it's *possible* that some nutty falconer around here might have released his bird to fly at an animal in a zoo. I don't *believe* this happened, I'm just saying it's possible. Of course an eagle would be really unlikely. It would have to be carried on the falconer's fist, protected by a thick leather glove, until the quarry was sighted at short range. The *buteos* are too large and relatively too slow to make the long diving kills of, say, the peregrine. No, it's *really* unlikely. Besides, where would the falconer have stood? In the middle of Fifth Avenue?"

"Maybe in the park?" he ventured. He glanced out the french doors. "Maybe from the terrace of a nearby apartment building?"

"Hardly. This whole speculation is preposterous, really."

Did she protest too much?

"Are there a lot of falconers around?"

"Not anymore. Guns pretty much killed the sport. I'd say there are only about two hundred and fifty in all of the U.S. and Canada...I suppose you could check with the American Falconers Association in Denver for the names of any around here." She shook her head. "Or then again, it might be the bootleg bird of an outlaw hawker. Not registered with any authority. This sport is regulated within an inch of its life."

"I realize your doubts, and respect them, but I think we may be on to something here—"

"I hope not," she said, and obviously meant it.

"You said before that sometimes a bird doesn't return to the hack," he persisted. "What does that mean?"

"Well, a good trainer will let a young hawk out on its own after a while to prey independently, building the bird's natural ability to take quarry. It's called being left at hack. Of course there's a risk involved—sometimes the bird doesn't return."

"So there are outlaw birds as well as outlaw falconers?"

She seemed annoyed. "Birds follow their own laws, not ours."

"Then a rogue bird?"

"Rogue? That suggests good and evil. Evil is a human invention."

Defensive again? he thought. "And here I thought it was invented by a creature with wings."

"What?"

"The rebel angel."

"You're chasing a fairy tale, David."

"Still, I think I'll check this out. I have little else to go on," he said, draining the martini glass.

"I'm going to have to kick you out soon," she said. "I have some work to do, have to put Guy to bed..."

"Sure, I understand."

An awkward few moments, and he was about to give it up and leave when she bailed him out.

"What branch of the service did you say you were in?" she asked.

"Air Force."

"Vietnam?"

"Do I look that old?"

She let it go. "Did you go to the Air Force Academy?"

"I was Air Force ROTC. At Columbia. Worked my way through," he added pointedly. Now who was being defensive?

"Why didn't you make a career of it?"

He was pleased at the personal nature of her questions. He pointed to his eyes. "Lousy eyesight. I wear contacts."

"What did you fly?"

"F-15. F-15 *Eagle*."

*   *   *

94

TORINO and his sister sat in the museum restaurant and ordered sandwiches. She drank white wine, he drank beer. She squinted at him over a baguette. "How's your love life, brother?"

Joining thumb and forefinger, he gave her a high-sign. "Picking up. Say a couple of novenas."

She looked surprised. "Who's the luckless creature?"

"So far it's a one-way street."

"Who?" she echoed.

"You don't know her. I don't want to jinx the thing."

She bit into the sandwich. "You gotta fight for it, kid. Ford mighty rivers. That kind of thing."

He nodded, recalling his own dragon-slaying reveries.

She reached across the table and touched his hand. "Scrap what I said about her being a luckless creature. I think you're the best catch in town."

"Okay, don't lay it on too thick," he said, "but I needed that."

"Have you mentioned it to mom?"

"I shouldn't even have told you. At this point it's just a gleam in my eye."

"Okay," she said. She pushed her plate away and touched up her lipstick. "I know I shouldn't do this at the table, but it's some trek to the powder room. How's the job going?"

"I have an odd case."

"Oh?"

"A red panda was killed at the Central Park Zoo. It was . . . disemboweled. Very strange business."

"Interesting. And awful. Any leads?"

"Well . . . not really."

AFTER Juliet had left, Torino stayed in the museum to use the pay phone and check in with Headquarters. He did not carry a cellular job, found it too cumbersome. No messages. He frowned, having half-hoped that Antonia would have called. He thought about Bannister and hated the thought. Admit it, you're falling for her.

On his way out of the museum something caught his eye and he stopped to examine it. It was a terra-cotta tablet from Mexico, Toltec art. Carved into the tablet was the image of an eagle. The bird was shown devouring a human heart.

Too much, he thought, and hurried on.

SOMEWHERE in the foothills of the Catskill Mountains, at the edge of the forest black with trees, lay the carrion of Red Bushnell. Clouds covered the sun and the earth was damp and cold. His eyes had been plucked like grapes by small birds. The bone-white husk of his flesh provided a bountiful meal for hosts of woodland scavengers. But the heart that once ached for Milly had already been consumed.

The hunter's jeep, well-camouflaged by the trees, would not be discovered for many more days.

Thirteen

AT DAWN THE hungry raptor rides the wind over Sandy Hook and the foam-scalloped waters of the Atlantic Ocean. The great head swivels to allow ice-cold eyes to survey the pygmy world below. She banks sharply, heading toward the Lower Bay and the Narrows. She knows winter and hunger and the taste of blood.

Long wings flap against a down draft as she passes over the shore of Brooklyn dominated by a large metal roost piercing the mists of morning, invading the eagle's domain of air. Thermals now rise from the concrete and stone below.

She uses her superior eyes. The double convex lenses zero in. The photosensitive rods and cones of the retinas send to the brain inverted color images of the objects caught by her great visual range. The nerve-endings pick up the inverted images and

*send them along the optic nerve to the base of the
brain where the images are stereoscoped, given
depth, put rightside up and consigned for memory
or action. She is primed by hunger for action.*

*She soars low over the bay and the span of cable
and steel that links land with land. Sunlight seeps
into the eastern sky. She ignores the craft that plow
the water below as within the scope of her fabu-
lous vision come places with names like Dongan
Hills and Bay Ridge, Hoboken and Highland Park,
Buttermilk Channel and Governor's Island.*

And Battery Park.

MURIEL Kramer, tears streaking her pancake makeup, anger
distorting her pixie-pretty features, minced over to the
closet and struggled into her silver-fox coat, pulled a matching fur hat down over bright red curls, stuffed stray ringlets
under it, placed hands on hips and turned to face her husband. Her complexion resembled that of a ripe tomato.

"I've had it up to here with you, you dimestore Casa-
nova," the words enforced by a slashing gesture to her
throat. She stuck her thumbs into the front pockets of her
Calvins. "What kind of a damn fool do you *take* me for?"

He stood by the window smoking a cigarette, gazing at
the wide black river, the dim forms of the skyline on the
opposite shore and the sky bleaching slowly with the coming of dawn. "Where do you think you're going?" he said.

"I'm going for a walk. I'm going to cool off. Maybe I'll
pick up some stud and have him screw my brains out."

He took the cigarette from his mouth and exhaled a long
plume of smoke. "Cool off? You'll freeze your sweet butt
in this weather. Come on, Muriel. Don't be silly."

She was pulling on her doeskin gloves, panting with anger

and effort. "I'll show you..." She muttered a chain of extravagant threats.

"Wait," he said, still in a flat tone. "The sun isn't even up yet."

"I want to watch the dawn."

"The sun rises in the east, Muriel. On this planet at least. The promenade faces west. You know, New Jersey? Kansas? California? West."

She was even more offended by the condescension and sarcasm. "I hope you get AIDS, I hope you get leprosy. I hope your damn dick falls off."

"Try to behave like an adult, Muriel, okay?"

"Don't take that tone with me, Marcus. I'm not one of your stupid self-centered junk-bond-peddling patients."

"Those patients paid for that fancy fur you're wearing, dear. Among many other things."

"Yeah, and they paid for those items from Harry Winston on your American Express card annual summary too, right? Which Wall Street bimbo did you buy those for? Or is it *bimbos*?"

He squashed out the cigarette in a green marble ash tray. The corners of his manicured mustache turned slightly upward. He shook his head. "Sneaking around like that, looking through my mail. That was childish of you, Muriel. Very childish."

"Oh... and you're a grownup, eh? A forty-year-old shrink entering the pussy-poking Olympics. You make me sick."

He sighed, as one might sigh at a child's innocent folly. "Let's go to bed, Muriel. We'll discuss all this later."

"Screw you? *Screw* you. I'm going out." She fumbled for her keys. "The next thing you hear from me will be in legalese."

"Suit yourself, Muriel."

"Suit yourself, Muriel. Tell me something, Marcus. I

mean, just as a point of like scientific curiosity. How does a cold fish like you ever get a hard-on?"

"I manage," he said with a smile.

She stormed out of the elevator into the lobby. The security guard was dozing at the desk. We could all get our throats slashed in our sleep, she muttered to herself as she exited the condo and stood shivering under the red canopy on Albany Street. She turned her head, looking first west, then east, then west again. She huddled into her coat and walked over cobblestones toward the promenade and Hudson River, leaning her shoulder into the whining, vengeful wind. She hated Battery Park City in winter. It was like living in an arctic weather station, she thought.

She pushed her way against the begrudging wind and sat on a park bench overlooking the hurrying river, its color changing with the dawn from black to battleship gray. She gazed through the black iron railing at the mist-mantled forms of the Statue of Liberty, Ellis Island, and the snow-capped towers of Jersey City and Hoboken. Screw him, she thought. Screw him a thousand times. And then she started to cry.

She opened her eyes, lashes webbed by tears. She called herself stupid for not bringing along tissues or a handkerchief. The clock of the red Colgate billboard in Jersey City showed 7:01. Why in God's name was she hung up on this philandering phony? Maybe she needed a psychiatrist. But he *was* a psychiatrist.

Dawn.

She rose and walked over the hexagonal paving stones toward the marina and ferry landing. The trees that lined the promenade swayed in the wind. She was alone. At this hour and in this weather, no joggers, no rollerskaters, no dog-walkers appeared. With her hands jammed into her pockets and the fur coat and hat covering almost every inch of her flesh, she could be taken for a sauntering animal. She passed shuttered restaurants and health clubs. No boats furrowed the surface of the water. Alone.

She reached the marina on Liberty Street, where a solitary yacht bobbed in the brackish inlet. She was a speck below the whitening domes and spires of the World Financial Center and the Twin Towers. Heaped buttresses of snow lined the walkway. She was miserable, her misery mocked by the wind. She made no plans, plotted no strategy of revenge, thought no coherent thoughts, just stood there taunted by the elements, letting emotion wash over her.

She heard bells, probably from the rigging in the marina. She huddled into the coat.

I'll fix his wagon, she thought, somehow I will . . .

She looked up, startled by the sudden murmur of a flock of pigeons mobbing in a frenzy over the dock. Again she heard a bell, not from the direction of the boat but from behind her. She turned. Her gloved hand covered her mouth as a cry of surprise and terror was smothered in her throat. The form of the thing overshadowed her. She heard the wind whooshing through the pinions. She saw the creature's tail splayed downward in a braking action and the talons lowered and outstretched. She saw a ruff of golden feathers ringing the fierce head, and she saw the red of the riveting eyes. And then only blackness.

In the liquid light of dawn the raptor strikes. Talons bared, she collides with the large silver animal whose scent and sight attracted her to the stony path on the edge of the river. The quarry falls to the ground. Quickly, precisely, the predator goes about her work, sinking claws down through fur and flesh, then, sated, she emits a shrill bleat and flies off until she appears as a circling speck in the milky morning sky.

TALONS

The body was discovered by a jogging bond salesman just after daybreak. In a cold sweat, he forced himself to use an outdoor pay phone to dial nine-one-one. He never jogged on that path again.

RAPTOR

Fourteen

IN LATE FEBRUARY a tantalizing whiff of spring came to the city. Casey, the derelict, washed his socks in Bethesda Fountain. Macaques groomed each other on boulders in the zoo. Pensioners played checkers on stone tables under still leafless trees. And, on the upper meadows of Central Park, little Guy Dunning operated a radio-control helicopter that lifted into the air as Antonia and Joe, sitting on a bench nearby, munched hot dogs. Above, a small red kite hovered on the wind.

Antonia looked at her companion. "He loves it, Joe."

"Yeah," said Bannister, "he's a damn good pilot for a three-year-old." Bannister really liked the kid, he just couldn't seem to get to first base with him.

Antonia seemed lost in her thoughts. She had not been able to get the ex-fighter-pilot cop out of her mind. He seemed to haunt her quiet transition moments, just before rousing herself out of bed, on the bus or in a taxi to the

105

office. It was extraordinary, this growing attachment to a virtual stranger. It was something she refused to name.

She said to Bannister, "It was good of you to get it for him, Joe."

"That's okay," he said, picking up a pebble and throwing it in the field.

She yelled at Guy, "Push the incline button, honey. The copter's heading for that tree."

The boy, sitting on his heels and gnawing his tongue in concentration, straightened the craft's flight pattern.

She turned back to Bannister, realizing how hard he was trying with Guy and not getting anywhere. She and the boy made a tight circle to crack, she realized. "How's the report coming?" she asked.

He frowned at the hot dog. "Slow as pouring catsup. Nobody meets deadlines anymore."

"Does New York stand a chance of getting ratified by— what do you call them—World's Fair Commissioners?"

"We stand an excellent chance unless..."

"Unless what?"

"Well, unless the city gets more than its usual dose of notoriety in the next few weeks and months. Bad publicity could really queer the deal."

"Hey, this isn't exactly Disneyland, Joe."

"I know." He continued throwing pebbles. "Part of the charm of living here, right? But I mean something real bad, not your run-of-the-mill rape or mugging or anything like that."

"Such as? Or shouldn't I ask?"

"Oh, maybe some sniper picking off every fourth person from the steeple of Saint Pat's. Or the Twin Towers turning into the twin towering infernos. I'm keeping my fingers crossed."

*   *   *

LIEUTENANT David Torino spent part of the diamond-bright day visiting the Native American Cultural & Historical Society in upper Manhattan where he managed to mine a few nuggets of information of doubtful use to the investigation. He learned that the cliff-dwelling Pueblos of the Southwest still keep birds of prey in captivity to use their molted feathers as ornaments and in religious rites. The Hopis of Arizona had federal permits to keep eyries and take the eyasses of the Golden Eagle. Farther south the Aztecs of Mexico, he learned, had had an elite soldier sodality called The Eagle, composed of fierce fighters who entered battle adorned with eagle feathers and skins and carrying shields with eagle insignia. Fascinating, except not too many Pueblos, Hopis, or Aztecs hung out in Gotham.

On the IRT Number 1 train rattling downtown he spotted a two-page story about a woman killed in Battery Park City. The details of the alleged murder of Muriel Kramer were interesting...

At the office he made a quick phone call to Detective Sergeant Andrew Catalano in the Squad Room of the First Precinct on Ericsson Place. They had been partners in a Ralph Avenue hell squad seven years before. They were never buddy-buddy—too different in personal taste and attitude—but they had survived a few tough scrapes together and turned over the same rocks. Torino sometimes even felt nostalgia for the Brooklyn tour.

"How you doing, wop?" said Catalano, employing his customary delicacy. Catalano was a Puerto Rican who passed for Italian, except when promotion time came.

"Fine-dandy, Andy," said Torino, wincing at the ritual banter. "And you?"

"They're hanging good, hanging good. What can I do you for?"

Torino got right to it. "Andy—you got the squeal on the Kramer case?"

"How'd you guess?"

"It's big so I figure they handed it to Andy Catalano." He meant it, too. The man was no diplomat, but he was a crackerjack gumshoe.

"So?" said Catalano, then added, "Hey, I know, you were boffing her, right?"

"Never knew the lady. But for reasons I won't go into right now I'm interested in the case."

"Don't try to horn in, partner. This is a juicy one and you already got your gold bar. Bust like this would put me over the top."

"Sure, Andy. Don't sweat it. My interest isn't yours." Which wasn't exactly true. "Can I ask a few questions?"

"Go ahead."

"Not over the phone."

"Okay, lunch. You're buying. Meet you at the Odeon tomorrow at one. It's halfway between your shop and mine."

Torino winced. He could have picked a less pricey place. "You got it," he said, and hung up. He took out his wallet and fingered his rarely used American Express Gold Card.

CATALANO told the waiter he would start with the artichoke and goat cheese appetizer, then have the cold poached salmon with endive, arugula and beets and would decide on dessert later. Torino swallowed hard and ordered the baconburger.

Torino inspected his ex-partner, who had grayed some around the temples since they last met, besides having put on weight. He knew how to deal *quid pro quo*, but he was a good cop and a good guy to have around when the stuff hit the fan.

"So," said Catalano, "it's your nickel, and then some

when you get the check. What do you want to know about the Kramer case?"

Torino knew it was a delicate situation; he didn't want to step on Andy's toes. "Prime suspect?"

"Now who do you think?" said Catalano.

"The husband."

"You know it's the husband. How long you been in this racket?" The plate of artichokes appeared and Catalano rubbed his hands together.

"Got anything on him?"

"They had a big row in public the night before she was meat loafed." He shook his head. "What a waste! She was choice, underline *was*." He began to eat.

"But you've got nothing on him?"

"Did I say that?"

"No."

"Okay, we got nothing on him. Yet."

"I read in the papers that he's a psychiatrist."

"Yeah, he's a witch doctor, all right. Wouldn't you know it? They're usually crazy." He drank beer and got a mustache of foam.

"The newspaper said she was stabbed. That right?"

Catalano scanned the dimly lit room for a waiter. The restaurant, formerly a cafeteria, had a Fifties-style decor, with formica, chrome and leather fixtures and wood venetian blinds screening the street. When he got the waiter's attention he tapped his beer glass for a refill. "Mutilated's the better word."

Torino's pulse pounded. "What do you mean?"

"I mean, she was practically disemboweled," he said, swallowing some goat cheese.

"What with?"

Catalano hunched his shoulders. "We're not sure. My guess is some kind of sharp gardening tool. The shrink has a summerhouse where he grows tomatoes and stuff. He also chases tomatoes." He nodded vigorously. "Don't worry. I'll nail the s.o.b."

Torino had to press him. "You mean you think he used a spade—"

"No. I mean one of those things that looks like a claw." Catalano wiped his mouth with a cloth napkin. "Hey, here comes your baconburger."

WALKING back to Headquarters, heartbeat quickening, Torino reviewed what Catalano had told him. He tried to keep himself from jumping to conclusions, aware of the snare of becoming overattached to a pet theory. He tried to avoid wild, premature speculation. He had to be the only person in the whole police department speculating on a connection between the killing of the red panda and the murder of Muriel Kramer. If anyone found out what he was thinking they'd probably write him off as a psycho. But he couldn't help it; things matched, no matter how bizarre the idea was.

Moving past a newly built skyscraper on Thomas Street, he realized he hadn't asked Catalano whether Muriel Kramer had been suffocated. So that was open. But other things fit too neat for comfort. The woman, the medical examiner had established, had been killed at daybreak. The detective made a mental note to ask Antonia something about this. Moreover, according to press reports, the victim had been wearing a silver-fox coat that had been shredded as well as her flesh. The weapon must have penetrated and mangled the coat before piercing the flesh. Wouldn't that have taken extraordinary strength? Torino crossed Broadway at Federal Plaza. Of course it was known that killers in the throes of bloodlust or anger were known to tap phenomenal reservoirs of strength. Torino didn't buy such an explanation in this case.

He was focused on the fur coat, and hat pulled down over the face. Couldn't she have been mistaken in the dim light of dawn for an animal? Of course he hadn't asked Catalano this. He wasn't ready to talk about his suspicion, except to Antonia. Mistaken for an animal by whom, or what?

He crossed Park Row, walked through a plaza and climbed the steps to Police Headquarters. He stopped on the pavement and huddled into his trench coat. It had grown colder again. A few paces away there awaited central heating and a hot cup of coffee. But somehow he felt compelled to stand there, looking around, taking stock. He gazed at St. Andrew's Roman Catholic Church and the Federal jail, juxtaposed like stage-managed symbols of good and evil. He saw the Greek revival colonnaded courthouses, the gray turrets of the Municipal Building ranging against the smoky white sky. Turning around, he saw the crusty green dome of the Woolworth Building and the huddled spires of the financial district. Here were the shifting peaks and valleys of New York City, formed by the plate tectonics of real estate. *Peaks and valleys.*

Could it be?

Fifteen

"EAGLES ARE CREPUSCULAR predators." He looked blank.

"They hunt at dawn or dusk, in twilight."

"Like fireflies?" Torino asked.

"I think fireflies are nocturnal," said Antonia. "So naturally, you can only see them at dusk. I'm not an entomologist, but I'm also pretty sure that they glow for sexual reasons, not as predators. Come this way." She led him up some steps to the upper part of the simulated rain forest of the zoo's so-called Tropical Zone, a climate-controlled interior space. Behind clear glass partitions all around them lived a variety of beasts, from leaf-cutter ants to pythons to piranhas.

He followed her up the steps, appreciating the rear view. "I see," he said, "fireflies glow to attract a mate."

"Something like that."

"Like human beings."

She ignored it, and he regretted the corn as soon as he

said it. When he reached her side on the landing she said, "Isn't it wonderful here?"

"Yes," he told her and meant it. "Where are the birds?"

"Look around," she said. She showed him thrushes, robins, tinamous and other tropical birds. They walked around, then stopped before an exhibit of caimans. "Beautiful creature, no?"

"Sure is, but I thought birds were your passion."

She looked at him. "Birds descended from reptiles, you know."

"From the serpent in the garden, eh?"

"I wouldn't put it that way."

Neither should he have. Cut it out, he told himself.

They continued through the mazelike exhibit. "I inspect all the zones and exhibits at least once a week."

"Yes." They stopped before a giant chuckwalla.

"He looks pretty nasty," Torino said.

Antonia smiled at the lumbering lizard. "Actually they're pretty harmless," she said. "Herbivorous. They have to watch out for us, really. Indians in the southwest eat them."

"Sure doesn't look like the salad-bar type."

"You'd be surprised. Nature always has tricks up her sleeve. For example, your romantic fireflies are carnivores."

"No kidding? What do they eat?"

"Earthworms, grubs, slugs."

They strolled through the steamy rain forest until they reached an exhibit of winged bats. "So," he said, "fireflies are carnivores...just like eagles..." It was a risk he had to take.

She stopped, hands on her hips. "I would have said like man. What are you driving at?"

"Just fishing around. The eagle hunts at dawn, right?"

She lapsed into academic—protective?—jargon. "As I've said, the golden eagle is a diurnal predator that normally strikes at daybreak, though she also makes her kills at dusk. Or at any time if starving or threatened. There'll be a quiz next week."

"Desi was killed at dawn, right?"

"Or thereabouts..."

He gazed at a cluster of bats huddled together and hanging upside down like fruit from a tree limb. "Why do bats hang upside down?" he asked.

"Because it's not easy to hang right side up."

Cool it, he instructed himself. You're going to make her angry, the last thing he wanted.

She saw his unhappy look. "I'm sorry for being short with you. I know you're only trying to do your job."

"That's okay," he said, relieved. "By the way, have you read about this woman who was killed on the esplanade in Battery Park City?"

"I heard something about it on the evening news."

"It's an interesting case," he said as they went outdoors and over to the Polar Circle where they saw gentoo penguins waddling around like a convention of portly priests reading their breviaries. "Would you like to hear some of the details?"

"If you think they're relevant."

"You never know about these things." He counted off some relevant facts on his fingers. "She was killed at dawn, she was wearing a silver-fox fur coat and hat, the coat, her flesh and organs were shredded by a clawlike instrument ..." He paused to let his words sink in.

She leaned against a railing. Of course she knew what he was driving at and a part of her wanted to shout that the notion was ludicrous. But in another part, fear grew like a belladonna in the dark. David's theory was outlandish—but possible. No escaping it. "I know what you're getting at, David."

"Isn't it possible?"

"An animal, yes, remotely possible. But a human being? No." The words were gritty as sand in her mouth.

"Let's look this thing in the face, Antonia. We can't be like the ostrich and hide our heads in the sand."

She gazed up at him. "The ostrich does not hide his head in the sand. He is scooping out a nest." At least she smiled when she said it.

"You are a wealth of information."

They buttoned their coats and went outside. Silently they watched the harbor seals, river otters, and polar bears frisking in the cold waters under the slate sky. "We have to be reasonable, David . . ."

He nodded, wondering if she meant reasonable about the killings or about the quiet growth of intimacy between them. They strolled on the wood walkway, close but not touching, gusts of cold breath intermingling.

"Where do we go from here, David?" He wondered too.

SHE had agreed to meet him for dinner, but first she walked back alone to the ivy-covered Arsenal. Joe would be busy tonight, occupied by a late press conference and work on the World's Fair report. She would have to call Mary and warn her that she would be home late. She went up the steps to her office, the brisk façade bristling with symbols of warfare—cannonballs, rifles, spears, swords. She knew the building was about 150 years old. It had served as an arsenal, a museum, a police station, a weather observatory. She liked its solid unpretentious utilitarian character. As she climbed the fourteen stone steps her mood was unaccountably light—until she looked up and saw above the steel doors and under a wooden crenelated molding the image of a warlike eagle, a ubiquitous symbol.

* * *

THEY dined at the Lion's Head in Greenwich Village, a cavernous bistro frequented by journalists. She had fish, he had chops. The food was good.

"What got you interested in birds?"

"Spitefulness. And rebellion, I guess. My father used to shoot ducks."

"It had to be more than that."

"Well, they're fascinating creatures. Endlessly fascinating."

Like you, he thought, but knew better than to say so. Not yet. Okay, then, to business. "Would you mind putting on the mortarboard again?"

"Go ahead, ask your questions, David."

"Don't birds winter in southern climates?"

"Depends. There's still a lot we don't know about bird migration patterns, and of course habits differ from species to species."

"Take the golden eagle, for example."

"Well, she's a far-ranging predator, large and strong enough to cover a lot of territory in search of food. Remember, food supply, not temperatures, is what determines migration patterns. Of course temperatures affect the availability of prey. Sometimes the eagle that nests in a mountain crag might migrate from a higher to a lower elevation rather than from north to south. There are a lot of variables. And the creatures don't always follow the script."

"In other words," he said, "they're unpredictable."

"They're predictable, but, well, an eagle might stray from the normal flight lane for some reason. Some ecological imbalance in the bird's normal winter habitat might force her to range pretty far afield in search of food." She hesitated before adding, "Also in winter the bird might be—well, less picky about prey."

"Meaning?"

116

She shrugged. "She'll go for whatever is available. And vulnerable."

"Including human beings?"

"*Excluding* human beings," she said. But her voice dropped a register when she added, "It might eat human carrion."

"Could the bird mistake a woman in a fur coat for an animal?"

"I very much doubt it, David."

"So, in spite of the art and folklore, raptors have never attacked man."

"I didn't say that..."

He waited.

"I believe there have been a few recorded instances..."

"Come on, Antonia, I know how you feel but—"

"All right, a few falconers, nomads in Central Asia. Training big birds like that to land on your arm involves risks. Even with all the protective covering they wear. Fencing masks, double-thick leather gloves. And then there's the great horned owl. I think this bird has been credited with attacking rangers in the woods of Minnesota."

"What happened to the rangers?"

"Blinded. Maybe one or two killed. But such instances are very rare."

Antonia got the waitress' attention and ordered a second glass of white wine. She seemed somewhat upset. "I wish I could say we had all the answers. You know, sometimes I think all animals are really beyond our ken. Like they're superior beings. There's so much we don't know..."

"We can speculate."

She looked away, into her past... "As a girl growing up in the Connecticut Valley I used to go hiking and I would see hawks and eagles migrate over the ridges, flying south. They came, I suppose, from northern Maine, Labrador, even

Greenland, following the crests of the north-south ridges, soaring on the updrafts. There would be a lot of them, especially after a cold front when more wind was bounced upward, creating the best flying conditions."

Torino recalled his days as a pilot. "Where were they heading?"

"A small high point on the Kittatinny Ridge called Hawk Mountain, on the border of New Jersey and eastern Pennsylvania. The birds were kind of funneled there by their instincts and the elements. In the old days people who called themselves *sportsmen* would congregate in the area to shoot birds." Her face was pale, grim. "Fish in a barrel. The rotting corpses of hawks and eagles would pile up at the foot of the mountain. Their wings were draped over roads, fences, even cabins."

"Does this kind of thing still go on?"

"Not at Hawk Mountain, the place is now a hawk sanctuary. But I ask you, who's the real predator here?"

Torino looked into her eyes, ice-green yet flickering with a kind of fire. "I have to ask you, Antonia. Is it *possible* for an eagle, a particular eagle, let's say, to develop a taste, a craving even, for human flesh?" He held his breath.

Slowly, with knife and fork, she separated white fish meat from bones. "Yes," she said.

Sixteen

EVERY ONE OF his family that Torino had invited over to his place for dinner thought he was nuts when he told them in confidence of his suspicion about the vicious killing he was investigating. Everyone, that is, except Dora Torino, the detective's mother. Like her only son, Mrs. Torino was tall and thin and had a long, rather melancholy face.

"I remember something. When I was a girl," she said slowly, her natural cadence when she was about to lapse into reminiscence. She had been born in a village in the foothills of the Dolomites, shadowed by the snowcapped Marmolada, surrounded by limestone beauty.

"Tell us, ma," coaxed her elder daughter Rose.

She looked abruptly at her daughter, surfacing from the depths of memory. "It was summer. We went to pick wild flowers, my friend and I. Her name was Cathi. She was fat and pretty. I always remember her." The old woman was sitting in a rocker by the wood-burning stove that David had brought back from a trip to Maine.

"So what happened, ma?" Rose prompted.

"It was late afternoon, near sunset. The mountains are so beautiful at this time, sparkling like jade. We stopped to have a bite. Goat cheese, wheat bread, *vino locale*."

"She can't tell a story without providing a menu," said Juliet.

"How old were you, ma?" asked Rose, as usual playing Sancho Panza in pursuit of historic truth.

The rocker creaked. "Ten, maybe."

"And you drank wine?" asked John, Rose's husband.

"Of course," said the old woman. "We sat in a meadow, the sky was dark blue with big gray clouds." She slipped into the present tense. "I see it like it happens today. After we finish to eat we sing a song, a mountain song. *Povre Filandere*."

"What *happened*?" Rose pressed.

Dora Torino glared at the older daughter. "Who tells the story?"

Rose sighed.

"*Beh*." The old woman's eyes became glazed. "It's a fascinating thing, what happened. We are about to turn back home when my friend, she points to an open space in the middle of the meadow. I look. A big bird, a hawk of some kind, swoops down and struggles with something in the grass, we can't see what. I hear the feathers rattle like when you shake a tree. Then the bird flies off, carrying the animal in its feet. We see it now, it's a hare. Not a baby but a full-grown hare. In the air he wriggles like crazy and tries to bite the bird but it's no good. My friend and I, we look at each other. We think it's all over but it's not. Suddenly the hare falls down from the sky. Then the bird lands on the animal and fluffs out its feathers, like a cape. Now the bird eats the animal, tearing at it with the crooked feet, then

120

the beak. When she finishes she cleans her beak on her feathers."

A moment of silence. "Well," Juliet said finally, "we asked for it." Torino said nothing.

LATER that night Torino lay on his back in bed, head cradled in his interlaced hands. He thought of eagles and Antonia. He wondered what it would be like to make love to her. Not a wise thought, not now. He thought of Wendy Belsen, an old flame. He was not cut out for long stretches of celibacy.

He forced himself to think of the case, particularly of the question he'd put to Antonia about whether an eagle might develop a craving for human flesh. Her answer surprised him. It had been qualified and speculative, but there was a history . . . She had told him the story of a famous German falconer named Jaeger who had trained berkutes by using children wrapped in wolfskin as lures. She had read that a rogue eagle had once attacked and killed one of the young boys the falconer had recruited from a Kirghiz tribe to play bait. After the incident the eagle, filled with a lust for human blood, never returned to hack and terrorized the people of the Alai valleys, attacking livestock, men, women, and children. Until it was captured and destroyed. She stressed that the incident was considered apocryphal by most experts and that even if true represented an extremely rare deviation from normal behavior.

Then he started thinking about his mother's story about the eagle who took the hare in the hills of Italy. The more he thought about it, the more his suspicion crystallized into a conviction. He knew he had to tell his boss Lee Goldschlager. He would have to risk ridicule, being taken for a psycho or worse. The situation was just too dangerous.

He put out the light and tried to sleep. He fluffed the

pillow, flopped from one side of the bed to the other. He couldn't get comfortable. In his half-sleep he heard the wind groaning through the open window. It sounded like the flapping of great wings.

FARTHER uptown in Greenwich Village in her penthouse eyrie Antonia Meadows listened to the late-night silence punctuated only by the sounds of her cockatoos, macaws and lovebirds. Nanook was at her feet. Mary and Guy were sound asleep. She thought about David Torino, not Joe. And as she massaged Nanook's neck and gazed through the greenhouse glass at the jagged masonry eyries of the city, darker thoughts came to mind. Was it really possible that somewhere, concealed in the concrete cordillera that ranged the boroughs of New York City, was the perch of a killer eagle? It *was* possible, and although her training and instincts rebelled at the idea of malevolence in an animal, her intellect did not. And if it were true . . . she tried to blot out the consequences . . .

Seventeen

TORINO GAZED OUT the window at the maze of viaducts that coiled around the exits and entrances of the Brooklyn Bridge. He had just told Lee Goldschlager his theory about the marauding eagle.

"So what do you think?"

"I *think* you must have picked up some rare illness down there on the fucking *pampas*."

"I went to Patagonia," Torino said sourly.

"Whatever." Goldschlager sat down behind his desk and squinted at Torino. "Look, I know you been dragging ass on this case but that doesn't mean you have to scrape the bottom of the barrel with wild theories."

Torino's face was burning with anger.

Goldschlager, realizing he might have gone too far, held up his palms. "Okay, okay, maybe I didn't mean the part about dragging ass, but, Dave, come on, a killer eagle?"

"It's possible, that's all I said."

"Hey, it's possible that Jimmy Hoffa's been impersonating the Pope."

"One question."

"What?"

"What if it's true?"

"What if *what's* true?"

"The raptor. The eagle."

"Take a vacation, Dave."

"I just got back from vacation."

"Then take sick leave."

TORINO needed air. Needed to think. On such occasions in the past he made a habit of taking a round-trip ride on the Staten Island ferry.

The boat furrowed the waters of the wide harbor. The squawk of sea gulls echoed in the concrete canyons. Torino leaned on the railing in the rear of the ferry and watched the skyline recede as the craft headed toward St. George. From this vantage, he reflected, the city sparkled with a falsely pristine light. He watched float by in the east the battered old fortifications on Governor's Island, then turned to gaze at the moldy green figure of Lady Liberty. The air was clear and cold. But his mind was muddled.

Ordinarily he was not a man given to prolonged bouts of retrospection and self-doubt. But now ... maybe he had let his imagination run amok. What *real* basis did he have for his suspicions about the raptor? A *feather*. The *testimony of a homeless alcoholic who heard bells*. He usually trusted his instincts as a detective. Now he wasn't sure.

The ferry slowed as it approached the Staten Island dock and the slopes of Fort Kill. As the boat disgorged commuters Torino stayed on board, basking in the bright sunlight of the winter afternoon, looking at Borough Hall and the sprawling old houses that hugged the crest of the hill. Soon, sideswiping the musty timbers, the ferry wended out of the landing and headed back toward the Battery. Maybe, Torino thought, infatuation had addled his brain.

Some four miles from the boat that carries the detective across the rippling surface of Upper New York Bay, somewhere amid the towers of Lower Manhattan that stabbed the achingly beautiful winter sky, high above the antlike throng and fisting masses of the financial district lies a great web of sticks decorated with boughs of fir and brush and pigeon feathers. And in this secret place a pair of yellow-ringed black eyes telescopes the outstretched city.

Antonia and Joe were browsing the stacks of the video store on University Place for a home video. They were in negotiations.

"Let's compromise," he said. "We'll rent an oldie but I get to pick it."

She showed him the jacket of "Ninotchka." "How about this one?"

"Seen it too often. Besides, the Garbo mystique has always eluded me."

They continued through the inventory.

"Here's one," he said, holding up the jacket of "Detective Story" featuring a pen-and-ink sketch of Kirk Douglas.

The title reminded her of David Torino. Earlier, in the taxi they had shared from downtown, she had told Joe about David's speculations on the killing of Muriel Kramer.

She nixed "Detective Story."

"Had enough of detectives lately?" he asked in what sounded like a hopeful tone.

She shrugged.

"Your friend has a vivid imagination," he added, pressing the point. "Let's hope he doesn't blab his theories around. I hate to think what would happen if some damn reporter got wind of such nonsense."

"What makes you think he'd do a thing like that?" not disguising her annoyance.

"Well, he blabbed to you, didn't he?"

"That's different." She hesitated, then added, "You're really worried about bad publicity for the city and what it might do to this World's Fair business."

"I sure as hell am." He started to say more, then checked himself and studied the jacket of "The Lavender Hill Mob." "Well, the police are convinced that the husband was behind the Kramer woman's killing. Not that he actually clawed out her guts but he put someone up to it."

"Have they got any proof?"

"No, but cops are always convinced that husbands bump off wives."

"Because they're misogynists with murderous thoughts about their own wives—"

"No. Because experience in such cases shows that murder usually is a family affair. Has been since Cain and Abel."

"Why would the husband have had her killed in such a gruesome way? Why not just get a hit man to stab her or strangle her or shoot her?"

"Hey, who can psyche a murderous shrink? Killers in general don't get high marks for rationality."

"The panda's death is still mystifying," she said uneasily.

"Yes. I hope to hell we don't have a maniac running loose. You know, some wrath-of-God loonie."

"Or some cult of killers."

He grabbed a jacket from the shelf. "Let's watch this one, it's a classic." He showed her "The Maltese Falcon," then was sorry.

The cassette cover showed the effigy of a black bird.

Eighteen

MARCH, CONFOUNDING THE almanac writers, reversed the tradition and came in like a lamb. Hannah Bright, an early riser, greeted the warm pastel dawn by stretching her body and smiling broadly, then bounded out of bed.

Hannah Bright, aptly named, was one of those rare persons who was quite satisfied with her lot in life. She had lots of reasons to be content. The daughter of a deceased banker and the widow of an equally deceased Anglican minister, she had no money worries and lived in a fine Federal-period townhouse on the bluffs called Brooklyn Heights. The house, she observed as she brushed her cranberry-colored hair, had a splendid view of New York Harbor, the Wall Street skyline and the Brooklyn Bridge. Though only four stories high, it was so strategically situated on Pineapple Street that no neighboring buildings deflected the rays of the sun in most seasons and at most times of day. She was pretty and had her share of elderly suitors with whom she toyed without taking them seriously. She was not old enough to be cranky nor young enough for the mists of *weltschmerz* that so often came over the unseasoned person. She had many things to keep her busy and give her a sense of fulfillment, including her painting, her work with the Municipal Arts Society and the Coalition for the Homeless, her column on urban gardening for the *Brooklyn Heights Express* and her rooftop garden of flowers, plants and vegetables, the envy of the neighborhood horticulturists. In fact the promise of good weather that had lifted her already cheerful spirits made her decide to go up to the roof this morning and prepare for spring planting. But first she had a few things to attend to.

She put on a red kimono and attached red curlers to her hair. Impishly she hummed, "The Lady in Red." Red was her favorite color. It had been a standing joke between her and her late husband Alfred that the minister's wife was a scarlet woman. When gray strands had begun to crop up in her chestnut-brown hair she went to the hairdresser and had it dyed red. She wore red lipstick and always painted her fingernails and toenails bright red. On canvas she liked to paint sunsets, sunrises and strawberry patches. She kept a mahogany-red Irish setter named Rusty. She liked to serve red snapper at formal dinner parties. And, like the Queen of Hearts, she cultivated red roses.

Lukewarm predilections did not suit Hannah Bright's style. She went whole-hog.

She went down to the kitchen and fixed herself tea and toast. After her usual morning stretching exercises, she fed the dog, put out the garbage and then climbed the spiral staircase to the roof.

The Golden Eagle lifts her broad dark-bordered
wings and spirals upward into the buoyant sky of

129

*morning. On shimmers of air she glides, over the
blotchy grid of rooftops and water towers, over the
narrow ladle of soupy water that separates the island of Manhattan from the deserted piers of
Brooklyn. Her beak clicks. Her breath mingles
with the warm sustaining air. She flies according
to the code bequeathed to her by a line of ancestral
birds tracing back to the Cenozoic era, flies as
winged atavus of future rulers of the air perhaps,
as strange as the pterodactyls that haunted the
jagged shores of primeval salt-water lagoons.*

*She flies, armed with beak and claws and great
strength, to form the latest link in the long genetic
chain of blood and beasts borne on air. She flies
after the essential thing—her quarry.*

*Soon she banks and brakes over Brooklyn
Heights, where her exceptional eyes are riveted by
splashes of red color on a roof far below.*

What a splendid morning, Hannah Bright thought, in-
haling deeply and surveying the cyclorama of city and water
views that stretched before her. Up here she had the feeling
of peace and seclusion, of unity with the sky and the elements that she supposed only people like, oh, Tibetan
monks in saffron robes experienced. She looked at the eastern sky, pink fading into blue. At this hour she heard only
the dim din of the city, the occasional honk of traffic and
rumble of helicopter motor, nothing loud enough to drown
out the comforting grumble of ledge pigeons and the twit-
tering of hardy wrens, or disturb the serenity of her temple
of growing things. Here it was her custom to wonder about
the existence of a personal God. She and Alfred had had
many talks on the subject. Priest, he was, but no stick-in-
the-mud dogmatist. She had long ago finished mourning

him but she still missed him. The loss of her husband did not shadow Hannah Bright's life; she was too fundamentally optimistic a person for that. Rather his death had colored her outlook with a patina of roseate sadness. It was a beautiful sadness, like the feeling evoked by sunsets.

But this was dawn and she was reflecting on the existence of God. When it came to church attendance Hannah went against the grain. As most people grew older they went to church more often. The minister's widow found herself going less often, although she still went often enough to keep up appearances and not scandalize the neighbors. She supposed that now her garden was her real church. While Alfred might not have approved, she believed that he would have understood this. As a lover of the miracles of propagation Hannah had an acute sense of the certain existence of a creative intelligence and all that. But she had little appreciation for the Judeo-Christian notion of a quirky patriarch who took a hunk of clay and fashioned Man in His own image. Oh, looking around at the modern world, she had no trouble conceiving of Man as created from *slime*. Her rose-colored glasses did not prevent her from seeing the darker side of human nature. But she felt no kinship to a Graeco-Roman deity with a curly white beard. She supposed that she belonged to that Kantian school of thinking that spawned the deists or transcendentalists or whatever one called them. Jefferson. Emerson. Thoreau. Whitman. *Walden* was her favorite book. She too wanted to "suck the marrow out of life."

A warm breeze wafted over the rooftops as thermals rose with the ripening daylight. As she walked over the terracotta roof Hannah Bright was absorbed in conjecture about how evil was reflected in the oversoul and other misty philosophical questions. These thoughts mingled with horticultural plans, repotting the red geraniums, planting new rose bushes, inventorying her material and equipment.

From the pocket of the kimono she produced a cluster of keys and selected one to unlock the potting shed.

Inside she turned on the light and looked around. She loved the aroma of the place, its reek of compost, leaf mold, dead flowers and drying manure. She imagined that this was how the Garden of Eden must have smelled in the dawn of the world. She scanned the corners and shelves. Plenty of loam, sand, perlite, peat moss, humus and crockery. She would need some bone meal, wood ashes, and charcoal. She made a mental note to order them from the farm and garden place that gave her a discount, not for having mentioned them in her column but for buying in large quantities. Of course she would need seed, and sprays and syringes for fighting diseases. She took no notes; her mind was photographic when it came to gardening matters.

Hanging on pegs on the walls of the shed were her tools, an impressive array of hoes, trowels, spades, rakes and other implements of many shapes and sizes. Watering cans and hoses were stacked in a corner along with planters and pots. She went over to a filing cabinet where she kept seeds. She opened a drawer and selected a couple of packets. She thought that she should change into her gardening clothes but she was too impatient to take the trouble, too eager to do something connected to bringing forth life in even a small way. Of course she was aware that the feeling grew out of her childlessness—Albert and she had discussed the matter thoroughly. She would plant the amaryllis bulbs in pots near the grape vines at the rear of the house. Off a peg on the wall she grabbed a hand rake and went outside. The sharpened claws of the rake glinted in the slanting rays of the early sun.

The raptor circles the house in the clear air. From her cloudless dawn-bleached vantage she sees the red animal amid the ragged landscape of stone escarpments and tar-paper plateaus, webbed bridges over calm gold water from Hell Gate to the mouth of the ocean. The city stirs and rivers crawl. She fastens her hyperoptic eyes on the crimson hair of her quarry. Then, like lightning to a metal rod, the creature falls.

The first thing Hannah Bright sensed was the overpowering stench. She heard bells. She turned and saw the two enormous outstretched black talons aimed at her throat. She tried to scream but as in a dream no sound emerged.

As the creature pounded her body to the surface of the roof, the victim grimaced in terror and stubborn anger and flogged her attacker with the rake.

Soon the terra-cotta tiles were stained with the red of blood.

Nineteen

DAVID TORINO HEARD the news from Catalano, who phoned him as he was reading a collection of poems by William Carlos Williams and listening to a Muddy Waters tape on earphones. He almost missed the call, since he could not hear the ring, but he happened to see the red light flashing on the console. Catalano had been notified by a colleague from the Eighty-fourth Precinct in Brooklyn.

"What's the matter?" said Catalano. "Don't you ever turn on the TV or radio?"

"Not too often. You say it was the same M.O.?"

"Identical."

Torino felt a rush of vindication mingled with horror.

"Let's see," said Catalano, "the victim's name is Hannah Bright, fifty-eight, a widow. Oh yeah, I forgot to tell you— she's still alive."

"Alive!"

"Barely. They got her in intensive care at Methodist Hospital. It's touch and go. She lost gallons of blood."

"Did she say anything to anybody?"

"Nothing coherent. A cleaning woman discovered the victim. She told Wilson at the Gold Street station house that Mrs. Bright was babbling some religious stuff when he found her. Something about a God of vengeance, stuff like that. Her husband was a minister."

"Nothing about her attacker?"

"Nah. Look, Dave—if anybody asks, it wasn't me who told you—but I understand they've collected some forensic evidence this time."

"What kind?"

"Not sure. Blood samples. Some other things. Remember, you didn't hear it from me. Everything's at the lab. If I hear anything more I'll let you know."

"Thanks, partner."

"Anything for an old pal. Take it slow."

"One more thing—how come they collected blood samples?"

"She fought back, it seems. Probably saved her life."

"She drew blood? How? With what?"

"With a gardening claw."

"Jesus!" Torino had an inkling that Catalano was holding something back. Even if the latest attack followed the pattern of the other two, this fact alone would not prove Torino's theory. He took a stab: "What else did they find, Andy?"

The other man's sigh was audible over the phone. "Mutes," he finally said.

Torino gave a puzzled look at the mouthpiece. "Mutes? What the hell are mutes?"

"Bird shit," said Catalano.

*　*　*

THE results of the forensic tests came back and a lid was clamped on the investigation. Reports were channeled in through headquarters computer center of similar attacks on a family dog in Rockaway Beach and a rube hunter near Phoenicia, New York. Both victims died. Antonia called Torino to tell them that she had been recruited by high city officials to act as a consultant in the case. Lee Goldschlager swallowed his pride and apologized to Torino for his sarcasm and skepticism. News that unnamed police sources were investigating the possibility that a murderous raptor was at large in the city had leaked to the press and stories credited to unnamed sources began appearing in tabloid newspapers, stirring a tempest at City Hall.

The mutes had hit the fan, Torino reflected.

Though he felt vindicated he was also horrified that his hunch had proved a reality. He learned that Hannah Bright's physical condition remained critical but stable. Police attempts to interview her were vetoed by doctors who explained that she was under heavy sedation and that she seemed to have suffered such serious psychological and physical trauma that she was incapable of rational speech in any case.

On Thursday morning Torino got a call from Goldschlager asking him to come to an immediate meeting at headquarters.

Entering Goldschlager's office, the detective stopped in his tracks at the sight of two men sitting there whom he recognized but had never met. One was Chief of Detectives Caesar Piccolo. The other man, leonine and self-assured, was Joe Bannister.

Goldschlager nodded at an empty chair. "Have a seat, Dave. I want to introduce you to—"

Torino stuck out his hand and said, "Don't bother, captain. I know who these gentlemen are. Pleased to meet you, Chief. Hello, Mr. Bannister."

Bannister took his hand. Piccolo, chomping on a cigar, nodded at the detective.

Piccolo, taking the stogie from his mouth, was the first to speak. "So you're the gumheel who came up with the eagle angle. My hat's off to you, son." The accolade had been given with a paradoxically sour expression. The chief had curly slate-gray hair and thick lips. He wore a wide tie with slanting red stripes. He puffed the cigar and swiveled jauntily in the leather-back chair.

"Thanks," Torino said. Keep it laconic. He flashed a look at Goldschlager. This was no time for I-told-you-so's.

"The lab tests support your theory about the raptor," Goldschlager said as he hefted a glass paperweight shaped like a bell. "We want you to head up the investigation, Dave."

Bannister stood up and paced the carpet. He made it clear that he spoke for Mayor Santiago. "We've got to find the damn bird."

"Why me?" said Torino. "I'm no animal tracker. Isn't this a job for the feds? What do you call it, the Fish and Wildlife Service?"

Goldschlager, Piccolo, and Bannister all looked at each other. "We'd like to keep them out of this as long as possible," Bannister finally said.

"Why?"

"There are...well, political concerns," said Bannister, leaning the heels of his hands on a window ledge behind his back. "You're aware of course that the golden eagle is an endangered species protected by federal and state law. You need a license to capture or even kill a depredating eagle."

"So let's get one."

"It's apparently not that simple," said Goldschlager.

"The problem is, can we trust the feds to keep this thing quiet?" said Bannister. "Some of the regional agents have close ties to environmental groups. Activists. Troublemakers. The Mayor doesn't want to spark demonstrations. A lot of these people are not exactly rational when it comes to killing threatened animals. We just don't want to take the chance."

Political gamesmanship, Torino thought. Mayor Santiago didn't want to tarnish his image as a supporter of conservationist causes in case he ever decided to run for higher office. Torino took stock of Bannister, his rival, whether Bannister knew it or not. He seemed smart, energetic, charismatic, and slippery as an eel. "Is worry about such protests the only reason we're to keep this under wraps?"

"No," said Bannister. "We'd also like to avoid widespread panic."

But, Torino thought, people had the right to know what they faced, the right to take precautions to protect themselves. It was a tough situation . . . the city was on the brink of the spring and summer tourist seasons. Millions, maybe billions could well be lost to the hotel, restaurant and related industries. He also remembered reading somewhere that the city was angling for approval as the locale for a World's Fair. No wonder Bannister wanted to keep it under wraps.

"I hear you were a fighter pilot. Ever see action?" Bannister was asking him.

"No. Too young for Vietnam, too old for the Persian Gulf."

"Well, I have a feeling you're going to see some action now."

Torino looked out the window at the crowded skyline and gray sky beyond. "Do we know whether the raptor was badly hurt in the struggle with Mrs. Bright?" he asked.

"Let's hope the thing's gone away somewhere to die," Chief Piccolo said.

"We can't count on that," said Bannister.

"I haven't the foggiest idea how to start the investigation," said Torino.

Goldschlager had a blackboard on casters in the office. He rolled it over to his desk. With chalk he drew a triangle and labeled its three points "Central Park Zoo," "Battery Park City" and "Brooklyn Heights."

"It forms kind of an isosceles triangle with two equal sides," Torino said, recalling the geometry courses he took in flight-training school.

"Right," said Goldschlager. "I'm guessing the nest is somewhere in the middle. On the basis of the attacks we know about."

Torino did not look happy.

"Don't worry," said Bannister, "you're not going to be working on this alone. We're teaming you up with an expert, an ornithologist. I believe you've met her." He looked more unhappy than Torino as he said it.

Torino suppressed a smile at the man's obvious uneasiness. Any misgivings he might have had about working on the case dissolved in an instant.

JOE Bannister sidled into the Mercury and instructed the driver to take him to a midtown hotel where the Mayor was giving a speech to the National Conference of Realtors. He thought about Lieutenant Torino. Impressive man, he had to admit, not your assembly-line flatfoot. He had plenty of qualms, though, about matching him up with Antonia to work on the investigation. He tried to put thoughts of the consequences out of his mind.

The draft report on the exposition had gone well. He had given it to the Mayor two days ago. But now this damn bird-of-prey thing had come up and the whole project was in danger of going down the tubes. When the news leaked out, Santiago had quickly called an emergency meeting of his kitchen cabinet. The Parks Commissioner had attended. The Police Commissioner, away at a convention, was ordered back to town. Bannister himself was instructed to defuse the controversy by downplaying the story to the press corps, hinting that the connection between the killings and the existence of the bird hadn't been verified. He also was ordered to disparage the tabloids that had carried the story as "supermarket scandal sheets."

Those at the meeting in the Mayor's private office were not overly worried... Sitting pols and their appointees were mainly damage-control specialists. Policy makers *reacted* to crises, most often situations uncovered by the news media. Unreported events, no matter how important or dangerous to the citizenry, were rarely crucial to the satraps of city government. Image was all, which made Joe Bannister, who shaped image, a star member of the scandal-busters. Deputy Mayor Breglio had asked him how much the story would hurt the bid for the World's Fair.

"Hard to say," Bannister had said at the meeting. "Best-case scenario, we keep the lid on the story and capture or kill the eagle. As of now the story is being ignored by most of the responsible news organizations. A couple of local television shows picked it up and treated it like a joke. It's in the 'killer bees' tradition."

But, Bannister now thought to himself as his car came off the exit ramp on the East River Drive, the danger sure as hell was real. In a few days a delegation from Paris would arrive to hear the city's brief to become the next World's Fair site. By then, he fervently hoped, the killer bird would be stuffed and mounted.

ON Friday morning the weather performed a quick-change from lamb back to wintry lion. Antonia shivered as she jumped out of bed to turn on the valves of the radiator in

her bedroom. She always turned them off at night before
going to bed because she found a cool room more conducive
to sleep. As soon as she heard the clang and clatter of un-
stopped steam she hopped back into bed. Her feet tingled
and her mind raced.

She was still stunned by the evidence that a great bird of
prey, an outlaw of its kind who attacked human beings, was
at large in the city. It fulfilled her worst nightmares of prej-
udice against animal predators, setting back the conservation movement fifty years. But she could not shut her mind
to the reality, and she had to respect—even admire—David's
intuitive powers. She also felt guilt for not having credited
the story sooner. And she felt a genuine fear. Not very ap-
propriate for a scientist, she told herself.

She folded her knees into her chest and rubbed her cold
feet, recalling again reading as a student the accounts by
the famous falconer Jaeger of eagles with killer instincts
soaring over the steppes of Central Asia and killing wolves.
If wolves, why not men? But how did the bird wind up in
this area? Thanks to DDT, guns, and the encroachments of
mankind, *Aquila chrysaetos* had been exterminated as a
breeding species in most areas of the eastern United States
for years. Well, the bird might have come from Canada or
somewhere around the Great Lakes. Maybe this holarctic
golden eagle somehow got deviated from a winter migration
flight over Hawk Mountain. She knew that raptors ranged
widely in search of food. Snowy owls, for example, had been
spotted at the city dump in Washington, D.C. And what
about the peregrines who lived in the tower of the St. Regis
hotel? Yes, she reflected, raptors were often found in odd
places. But to attack human beings? A *rara avis* indeed.
Reported attacks on humans in the past were always defensive and accidental. Say, a falconer without a fencing
mask. Or a hunter wearing a fur cap. This thought renewed
her respect for David's deductive abilities. Muriel Kramer

had been wearing fur. And Hannah Bright's red curlers must have resembled red meat to the high-gliding eagle. Which suggested an interesting conclusion: the bird, indeed, had been trained to the lure, *with butchered meat as bait*. She made a mental note to share this theory with David when he arrived for their breakfast conference this morning.

The room had warmed up, so she got out of bed and headed for the shower.

DAVID arrived promptly at nine-thirty. Mary had already bundled Guy off to nursery school and was visiting a friend. They acted nervously with each other. It was not lost on either of them that they were alone together in the apartment. But over coffee and croissants in the alcove overlooking the terrace they became more relaxed and focused on the business at hand.

She told him about her conclusion about the hair curlers.

"Makes sense," he said. "You know that the raptor's injured?"

"Yes."

"We're not sure how bad."

"A bird of prey who has lost blood heads straight for water to replace body fluids. Chances are she survived the struggle. Birds of prey have remarkable—one might even say miraculous—powers of recovery. Their bones set in about three weeks. And they're not subject to infection like us mammals."

"That's scary. Why is that?"

"We don't really know. Something to do with their higher body temperatures."

"It always surprises me how little scientists and doctors know."

"Me too," she said. "Anyhow, raptors often recover very quickly from rather ugly-looking wounds. I remember a

142

Haliaetus at Cornell that had been shot by a farmer in the underwing coverts. Looked bad, but she recovered in a few days."

"What is a *Haliaetus*?"

"I'm sorry. Species *Haliaetus leucocephalus*. The common American bald eagle. It's the only eagle restricted to America. I think that's why it's our national symbol."

"It's related to the golden eagle?"

"Not too closely. Same subfamily, different genus. They're fish eagles. The American eagle is not a true eagle, an *aquila*. The golden eagle is."

"Can they interbreed?"

"Of course not."

"Not even like a donkey and a horse?"

"No."

Or an Italian and an Anglo-Saxon? he thought but didn't say.

She seemed to sense where he was going and promptly launched into a lecture on where the raptor might be nesting. "By instinct," she said, "they build stick nests in remote inaccessible places. Sometimes in caves. More often on the sheer faces of cliffs."

"In skyscrapers?" he asked.

"It's possible. What *aquila* wants most in a nest is what a lot of New Yorkers also want—a commanding, unobstructed view. But not, of course, for aesthetic reasons. She must see the surrounding terrain in order to hunt."

"You know, in the Air Force we were taught to study the enemy, to know him intimately. Exactly what are we up against here? How strong is this raptor? And how smart?"

Antonia's face tightened. She did not like to think of any bird as the enemy. "Well," she began reluctantly, "judging from the slice they found at the scene, this was an unusually large bird of prey."

"Slice?"

"It means the same as mutes."

"Oh, bird shit."

"If you like. The Brooklyn detectives told me they found very long splashes of whitewash on the roof. Incredibly long."

"A giant bird?"

She shrugged. "I wish I'd had the chance to see it. They took specimens and cleaned the rest up."

"An ordinary golden eagle can be pretty formidable, right?"

"Absolutely. Especially one primed by hunger."

"I know that they use their talons. Do they bite too?"

"Yes. But their feet are the most dangerous weapons. An eagle's claws are larger than a lion's canines. And coming at you from a long stoop much stronger."

"Okay, they're strong. How smart are they?"

"We don't really know how to measure human intelligence, much less bird intelligence."

"What does your experience tell you?"

Her fine skin seemed slightly moist. Was it on account of emotion over the subject or something else? She took a while before answering the question, collecting her arguments. She leaned across the table. "Consider this, David. Eagles in the Hebrides hunting sheep in flocks use teamwork. Two, sometimes even three birds cooperate against the quarry. While one eagle distracts the attention of the ewe, another will attack the lamb and carry it off. Is this intelligence or so-called animal instinct?"

"They carry?"

"Falconers discourage the habit but they sometimes do. Large eagles have been known to carry off to their eyries animals weighing as much as eighteen pounds."

"The myth of Ganymede," he said with an air of discovery.

"Yes, cup-bearer to the gods." She drained her coffee cup.

"Here's another example of avian intelligence. Herring gulls carry clams in their bills and dash them on the rocks below in order to eat them. A skeptic would say that the gulls didn't think this out but merely followed their instincts or imitated their parents. That some primeval ancestor gull discovered the technique by chance. Sounds like the invention of the stone axe and the wheel, doesn't it? Chance discoveries of a primeval ancestor later used in a pattern of inherited intelligent behavior."

"So I gather you believe the raptor is one very smart bird."

She rocked slightly in the chair, considering. "You know, we humans confuse high technology with intelligence. If only we could inhabit the essence of animals, get inside them. I think we'd be shocked to learn how many of the distinctions we treasure in our little minds—the differences between intelligence and instinct, mind and body would become meaningless. Would molt like feathers in summer. Sorry, I didn't mean to get mystical on you."

Her face was tinged with color now.

He shook his head. "Don't apologize. There is a Catskill eagle in men's souls ... "

"What's that?"

"A line from *Moby Dick*. I think."

From the greenhouse came the yawp of a cockatoo, which seemed to bring them back to the business of working out a course of action. Their main objective was to locate the raptor's nest. Torino suggested using police helicopters to search the canyons of the city. Antonia said it was illegal to hunt down eagles by aircraft. As they talked and planned he resisted what he felt about her, and she felt uncharacteristically awkward when making an analytical point.

But whatever their plans, they quickly would be outstripped by events.

Twenty

DENNY MORAN KNEW he was rushing the season. But he was an addict and addicts had no will power. At the first breath of spring he had to answer the siren call of his fishing boat *Circe*. He left the old lady crabbing about visiting her mother in Kew Gardens because any day now she would be pushing up petunias in Maple Grove Cemetery, climbed into the old Chevy Nova and took the Shore Parkway toward bliss.

It was still pretty cold, he thought, cruising past the Bay View Houses of redolent Canarsie (where he kept sugar on the side), but bottom fish like cod and blackfish would probably be biting this time of year and anyhow the catch was not as important as the quest. The vehicle swayed in the sail-snapping wind that came off Jamaica Bay.

He passed Marine Park, Mill Basin and the undulating reeds of Plum Beach. Looking south he could see the spires of high-rise apartments across the bay at Breezy Point and savored the prospect of sailing beyond them to the mussel beds where the fish were waiting. He hoped.

Displaying his police credentials on the windshield, he parked the car in an illegal spot on Emmons Avenue in Sheepshead Bay just a few paces away from the slip where he kept the boat. From the car trunk he retrieved his cooler and gear, including sinkers and stiff seven-foot rod with 4/0 Penn reel loaded with a forty-pound test. He bought clams at the bait shop and was ready to roll.

At sea he cast the line, sat in the deck chair, popped open a brew and drifted toward Nirvana. He was only a couple of miles off Rockaway but he might as well have been in Fiji. In his twenty-six-foot Mako on the breast of mother sea Denny Moran found inner peace. Here the quacking of his wife Josephine receded into oblivion. Here memories of the vermin who infested the Sixty-first Precinct on Coney Island Avenue sailed into the mist. He thought about using the Loran and motoring out farther offshore to locate wrecks but nixed the idea. March was unpredictable and a sudden squall might materialize. He was content to angle for open-bottom fish. After all, he was in no hurry, he had two six-packs and plenty of bait.

It happened as he was polishing off his fourth beer. He was hauling in what felt like a twenty-pounder (he could see the gray-green scales glinting in the sunlight) when seemingly out of nowhere it swooped down to steal the fish.

The cop blinked in disbelief. At first he thought it was a giant petrel of some sort but it was too dark in color and larger than any petrel he had ever seen. In fact it was the largest flying bird Denny Moran had ever seen on land or sea. And the most ferocious looking.

The creature mantled its brown primaries over the fish, struggling to free it from the hook. Moran, gazing dumbstruck at the scene, swallowed hard, then remembered reading something in his favorite tabloid. "Sweet mother of Jesus," he said.

He moved quickly. He secured the fishing rod and fumbled in a canvas bag for his service revolver. Gluing his eyes to the great bird, who by now had freed the prey, he manacled the wrist of his shooting hand to steady it and squeezed off a shot.

Fish clasped in crooked yellow hand, the bird already had caught an updraft when the bullet struck its abdomen. The beast plunged toward the scalloped waters, flapping mightily, gained altitude, then flew toward the misty shore. The cod had plopped back into the water.

Cursing, Moran turned the ignition key. "Winged the son-of-a-bitch," he said as the boat purred back toward Sheepshead Bay.

CASEY, turtling into his coat collar against the chill, walked north on the Mall past the bandstand. His mouth felt bone dry and his head ached from the effects of yesterday's sweet wine. He was heading for Bethesda Fountain and his morning wash-up. It would revive him a little before setting out to panhandle enough change to buy another taste of oblivion. He looked at the sky where a smoky sun rose to just clear the tops of the Fifth Avenue high-rises and splash the grayness with gold. He slogged over the pavement on the cracked soles of well-worn army boots.

He stopped to rest at the north end of the Mall at the top of a grand flight of stone steps leading to a wide plaza at the rim of the lake and boathouse bobbing with small dinghies. He gazed at the landscape. This was the center of Central Park, a place that evoked a picturesque past, a time that would never return. There was a stone bridge curving gracefully over the lake, the castlelike weather station on the hill overlooking the Delacorte Theater and Shakespeare herb garden. Beautiful Bethesda Fountain.

Casey rubbed his mottled eyeballs and looked again. Could he trust his senses? He hadn't drunk a drop in hours. Nobody else was in the area. Casey froze like the surrounding statues.

There she was, using the fountain as a gigantic birdbath. The creature was sepia-colored, the hackles on the head and neck filigreed with gold. She feaked her black beak on her wing feathers. The bird had dry yellow cere around the nostrils and two glaring black eyes circled with yellow. She was feathered down to the yellow toes and black talons now immersed in water. The forked black tongue flickered to her wounds. Then she spread the great canopy of her wings to an incredible length and with a powerful downstroke mounted toward the sky.

Casey leaned on the balustrade, gasping for breath. What devil bird or evil angel had ascended from the hood of Hell? He sat on the steps for a moment. When fear finally loosened its grip on his chest he got to his feet and ran, like hell, in the opposite direction.

THEY could no longer keep it quiet.

The headlines trumpeted the news to a frightened populace: "Raptor at Large"; "Giant Bird of Prey Sighted in City. Police Probe Link to Recent Attacks on People & Panda." The phone lines at police headquarters and the city hall press office were jammed with calls from around the nation, and the world. At dawn and dusk many streets that normally teemed with people now looked like no-man's-land. Some people bolted their windows and kept their kids home from school. More often, though, they joked—nervously—about it in neighborhood bars and shopping centers. Disbelief tended to prevail and people went about their business, trusting the word of most public officials who advised against panic, portrayed the reports as exaggerated and predicted that, at any rate, the injured bird would not survive the stabbing and gunshot wounds.

So far silence from City Hall, where the Mayor and top advisers, including Antonia Meadows and David Torino, were meeting to plan strategy for an upcoming press conference in the Blue Room. They had before them printouts of interviews with witnesses who reported sighting the raptor, including the cop Denny Moran and Casey Brown. The composite picture of the creature that the witnesses painted was consistent and hair-raising. Some officials even wondered whether some kind of mass psychosis had not possessed them to generate such tales of a winged Gorgon. Indeed, Gotham was a city proverbially known for the folly of its inhabitants.

But Antonia knew that this was neither folly nor mass hysteria. This was, unfortunately, for real.

A breeze through the open window of the Mayor's office made the ceiling chandelier chime. Antonia frowned at Santiago's conjecture that, using his malaprop, "The bird is a dead duck." She interrupted him to explain about the golden eagle's immunity from infection and remarkable recuperative powers.

"The eagle was replenishing body fluids in the fountain," Antonia said. "I don't believe the bird will die from the wounds."

All eyes were on Antonia—Santiago's, Helmut Frank's, Breglio's, Piccolo's, Police Commissioner Duren's and, of course, David Torino's. Only Bannister did not look at Antonia; he was watching Torino.

Breglio asked her to explain the bell and strips of leather that reportedly were tied around the raptor's feet. She told him they were equipment used by falconers, the bell to locate lost birds, the jesses for attaching a swiveled leash.

"So this here's a tamed bird, not a wild one," Santiago said.

"Let's just say the eagle once probably belonged to a falconer. I hesitate to call a golden eagle tamed. There's always a feral streak in the bird's nature, one that the falconer merely exploits rather than domesticates. The falconer shares the sense of quarry, plugs into it."

Breglio returned to his earlier question. "Then these jesses, as you call them, they're like reins on horses, right?"

"They're the devices the leashes are attached to. As a matter of fact, they predate reins on horses."

"In other words," said Breglio, "this is an escaped bird?"

"Some might say liberated," she replied.

Joe Bannister didn't like what was brewing. He had enough troubles, what with the upcoming visit by the French delegation. At a breakfast meeting earlier a representative of the Association for a Better New York had predicted to him that the situation would set the tourist business back ten years. Meanwhile the feds had been breathing down the Mayor's neck to make sure that they went through proper channels and did not violate federal law in their attempts to capture the raptor. They didn't want an open season on an endangered species. Over the phone the regional director of the Fish and Wildlife Service in Boston had told Bannister that the city needed a depredation permit to even "take, possess or transport" a depredating bird, not to mention kill one. Application for the permit required them to describe where the so-called depredations were occurring, what kind of crops or "other interests" were being injured, the extent of the injuries and so on. Killing predators entailed another set of rules and regulations and even more red tape. The eagle could be killed "only with a shotgun not larger than No. 10 gauge fired from the shoulder, and only on or over the threatened area or area described on the permit." The law also banned use of blinds, pits, other means of concealment, decoys, duck calls or such luring devices to entice the predators within gun range. Bannister was told that certain exceptions to these rules might be authorized but only after providing evidence of the need to suspend the regulations and only after a time-consuming application procedure.

"The permits are issued for no longer than a year," Bannister told the group in the Mayor's office.

Santiago looked at Bannister. "Can't we tell the feds to cut the bullshit? This is a goddam emergency—"

"I'm trying my best," said Bannister. He left unsaid what everyone in the room knew—there was no love lost between the federal bureaucracy (in the hands of Democrats) and the Republican regime occupying City Hall. And they could count on little help from the Governor's office and the legislature in Albany, the one also in Democratic hands, and the other always hostile to the big city.

"Killing a golden eagle is a serious matter," Antonia said.

"So's killing people," observed the Mayor.

"I *realize* that, and I'm not against killing the raptor if it comes to that."

Santiago told the group, "We've decided to cooperate with the federal authorities to the fullest degree possible. We'll tell that to the press." He smiled at Antonia. "We will even try to take the bird alive." He looked at the Police Commissioner: "Without risking the lives of citizens, of course."

Bannister said, "The Director is expediting the depredation order. They do it by publication in the federal register. Only persons named on the permit are authorized to take the bird." He looked around the room. "Who's it going to be?"

"Ms. Meadows and Lieutenant Torino—naturally," said the Mayor. "A cop and a zoologist." Bannister read between the lines: the choice designed to please the conservationists on the one hand and a frightened populace on the other.

152

"Okay," said Santiago, "here's the deal. We search every nook and cranny of the city infrastructure. Bridges, towers, skyscrapers, tall trees in Jamaica Bay or Staten Island. Every inch. We look for the nest or the eyrie or whatever the hell it's called. Either we chase the thing away or kill it, or capture it. If we capture it we hand it over to the feds. Ms. Meadows will tell us where to look and how to predict the bird's behavior. Torino here will carry a shotgun. Just in case."

Twenty-one

Word came from Methodist Hospital that Hannah Bright's condition had improved enough for her to talk briefly. David Torino called Antonia Meadows.

In the cab going down Broadway toward the Brooklyn Bridge he filled her in on his previous day in a helicopter searching the city and its environs for the raptor's nest. He'd carried both a shotgun and a tranquilizing gun. "Needle in a haystack," he muttered.

"Yes," she said, "even such a large bird might be hard to locate. The eagle has an extended territory, ranging far in search of quarry. She's a powerful flier... Did you search the Palisades?"

"Sure did. We covered all five boroughs, Jamaica Bay and Long Island plus parts of New Jersey. We didn't go as far up the river as Bear Mountain. Could the eagle come from that far?"

"I doubt it." She looked grim. "Judging from the location

of the attacks I think she's more likely nesting somewhere in the city."

"Antonia, why do you keep calling it 'she'? Couldn't it be a male?"

"I suppose so. It's a feeling I have. No, it's more than that ...in all birds of prey the female is larger than the male. Sometimes a lot larger. Also, a lot more deadly."

A hospital administrator ushered them down a long corridor toward Hannah Bright's private room. At the door the official, a plump woman with artificially colored auburn hair and wearing a purple suit, stopped them. "She's still very weak and in a serious condition. Please make it as brief as possible and don't tire her."

Hannah Bright's hair formed a red corolla on the white linen of the pillow. An intravenous tube stretched from her arm. She was dozing.

Antonia and David stood there trading awkward glances. Finally he gently nudged the patient on the shoulder. Her eyes fluttered open.

"How are you feeling?" Torino asked her after introducing himself and Antonia.

"Lucky to be alive," she told him.

They sat on the hard chairs and looked around. The room was filled with baskets of flowers of all colors and kinds— geraniums, roses, glads and mums.

Hannah said, "My friends know how much I love flowers."

Her voice was frail but distinct. Her face was unmarked but her shoulder was heavily bandaged as well as parts of her body covered by the bedsheet. Her injuries had been severe, the doctors said, and she had lost much blood. She had been given massive transfusions of plasma and treatment for trauma.

"We've been assigned to your case," Torino said. "Ms. Meadows is a scientist, an ornithologist. We'd like you to tell us as much as you can about the attack. To help us ... capture the bird. We realize how painful recalling it might be for you."

"I doubt it," she said. "Not even Dante could have imagined such a hellish creature."

Torino asked, "Can you describe it?"

Recollected terror glazed the patient's eyes. "It was a nightmare, only it was real." She stretched out a mottled hand. "As real as this hand." She shook her head, as if to shed the memory.

"How big was it?" asked Torino.

"Bigger than any bird *I'd* ever seen, like something from the pages of a grotesque fairy tale."

"Can you remember anything about its wing span?" Antonia asked.

She shook her head. "I was fighting with the damn thing. Fighting for my life ... "

"Of course," Torino said quickly, "we understand. Anything else?"

She squeezed her eyes shut. "I still have nightmares about them."

"Them?"

"The claws, but I fought it off. I don't know how ... "

"Did the eagle make any sounds?" asked Antonia.

"Was it an eagle? Yes, now that you mention it, it looked like an eagle or maybe a giant hawk. No, no sounds that I can remember. Except for the bells."

"You heard bells?" Torino said, and looked at Antonia.

"Yes. It must have been wearing a bell somewhere on its body. Oh, and leather straps around the feet."

"Go on," said Torino.

"And I remember there was a smell. An *awful* smell." The woman was breathing heavily now, her cheeks flushed.

156

"Smell?" said David, glancing questioningly at Antonia, who looked grim.

The administrator was back into the room then. "You're upsetting her," she told them. "You must leave now."

Before they left, Hannah Bright suddenly grasped Antonia's wrist. "You know," she said, "before it happened I'd been thinking about things...I mean, well, I'd been questioning God, whether there was one..."

"I guess you believe now?" said Antonia.

The woman shook her head and her red hair splashed the white pillow. "I don't know. But I do know one thing—I now believe in Satan."

She was dead serious.

OUTSIDE on the street in the stinging wind they walked without speaking down Sixth Street in the direction of Prospect Park, past brownstones and Victorian street lamps and yapping dogs. In the park, near the bicycle paths and picnic area that surrounded the old Litchfield Mansion, now Borough Headquarters of the Parks Department, Torino finally broke the silence. "One thing I don't get—this business about the smell. What was that all about?"

Antonia looked grim again, as she had when Hannah mentioned it in the hospital room. She took a deep breath. "Well, I remember hearing falconers and zoo-keepers mention the way the breath of raptors smelled under different circumstances. Nobody *really* knows why, but the breath of tame birds has a rather sweet smell while the breath of fresh-caught wild birds reeks pretty badly."

"What causes it?"

She shrugged. "Some experts speculate that a muscular change takes place in the bird's body that gives off the smell of the stomach contents."

"And what causes that?"

"Fear, stress, injury. There are all kinds of theories. I have my own."

"Which is?"

"I think it's plain old hunger," she said.

ANTONIA hadn't quite realized David Torino's effect on her until she was finally alone later that day after a lousy tennis match with her friend Rachel and some badinage about her love life. Her attachment to Joe Bannister was still there, and still exclusively physical. She sensed that her attraction to David was something of the same, but more. Which confused, worried . . . and excited her.

Twenty-two

THE SKY ABOVE the man-made granite cliffs is often filled with the clatter of big steel birds with wings that turn round and round. They are strange and fearsome creatures in the raptor's eyes. They intrude upon the place where the sturdy stick nest was built, stirring up territorial instincts. They disrupt the hunt and the roost. They kindle the vital impulse of the raptor to defend the home.

Such a metal bird has invaded the range of the raptor often lately, raising the hackles of war. She waits.

THE chopper's blades chattered intrusively, a loudmouth in a cathedral.

The city below was a winking jewel of many facets, the surrounding sky an inverted bowl on a potter's wheel, ranging in color from powder blue in the east to brick red in the west. From the air at dusk in early spring New York City appeared fabular, the clustered turrets of a new Troy.

"What's that down there?" Torino said, pointing in the direction of the Verrazano-Narrows Bridge.

The pilot, Police Officer Arvin Taylor, sighed. Most likely another false alarm, he thought to himself. But he wasn't about to complain to a dude sporting gold bars.

"We'll take a closer look," said the pilot, lowering the collective pitch lever to make the aircraft descend. Simultaneously he pushed the right rudder pedal, pointing the helicopter toward the bridge and the object hovering near it in the twilight air.

The helicopter bobbed and pitched, making it difficult for Antonia to focus the binoculars. The pounding of her pulse didn't help matters. All she could see was the wrinkled surface of the bay and the spires of the suspension bridge.

Finally, though, she managed to zero in on the flying object. "Forget it," she said glumly from the back seat of the Jet Ranger.

"What is it?" David asked.

"A kite in the shape of a thunderbird," she said, training the lenses on the kite string and tracing it to the hand of what appeared to be a young boy in Fort Hamilton Park.

"How many kites does that make?" David asked with a weary sigh.

"Who's counting?"

Taylor reached between his knees to raise the pitch lever and tilt forward the control column, making the helicopter continue south over Gravesend Bay.

Torino saw a faint smile on his face. Sure, what did Taylor care? He was making a fortune in overtime. Day after day they had flown, at dawn and dusk and in between. They had had nothing but false alarms every time they had taken off from Hangar Four in Floyd Bennett Field in Brooklyn. They had chased sea gulls, promotional balloons, small aircraft, windblown garbage bags and kites. Everything airborne, except the raptor. Maybe they needed some special trick to lure the creature out into the open. They couldn't just rely on serendipity.

The detective took a drink of iced tea from the thermos, thinking that he could really use a cold beer. His contact lenses were making his eyes water. The shotgun lay like a dead weight in his lap. Glancing periodically at Antonia helped some, even though she seemed gloomy and preoccupied. But her eyes still sparkled. She was wearing bluejeans, a safari jacket, olive-green shirt and foulard scarf. Today her hair was worn loose, spiraling wildly in the wind.

The blue-and-white chopper now scuttled sideways toward Queens.

"Shall we pack it in?" asked the pilot, a cheerful man with a mocha-colored baby face that contrasted with the grains of gray in his hair.

"Not yet," Antonia said. She had not asked Torino's opinion, the detective noted. "There's a few minutes left before nightfall. And... well, I don't know... "

Torino, studying the instrument panel and steering devices operated by Taylor, thought about how helicopter piloting still very much depended on the skill of the person at the controls instead of the sophistication of the equipment, like in flying supersonic jet aircraft. In fact, the helicopter, since the wings, the rotors, were moveable, more closely imitated the bird in flight than fixed-wing planes. A helicopter, like a bird, didn't need a runway for takeoffs and landings, and also like a bird, could fly straight up and down, forward, backward and sideways, and even hover in the air. And its disadvantages were like a bird's—it lacked the speed and altitude of other aircraft and required frequent refueling. After all, the helicopter had been invented by Leonardo, that consummate student of nature and her aerial artists...

He looked back at Antonia, who was staring straight ahead, combing back her chestnut hair with her fingers. "We've got to find her," she muttered, the tranquilizer gun gleaming metallically on the seat beside her.

Torino thought he understood why she had been adamant about coming with them on the hunt. She mistrusted everyone, including him, to avoid killing the raptor if at all possible. How wrong was she? He was sure that people like Santiago and Bannister, while paying lip service to the idea of conservation, would rather that the eagle and the problems she brought be dispatched with as little fuss as possible. In a way it was hard not to sympathize with this point of view. She was, after all, a bloodthirsty killer. He could understand Antonia's reluctance, but *this* eagle was definitely an outlaw, a black vulture.

He saw Antonia's expression suddenly freeze. The binoculars covered her eyes. "*Look,*" she called out, pointing downward.

Low in the great open space over Gravesend Bay something flew. It had broad straight wings, slotted primaries and a stately wingbeat that suggested great power. Large-clawed feet dangled from the body. The head swiveled from side to side.

"Aquila," she said in a dry, metallic tone of voice. "Adult plumage. This may be it..."

Taylor's habitual grin dissolved. He lowered the lever and tilted the control column. The helicopter swooped downward.

Torino patted the shotgun. His heart pounded.

As the helicopter approached the bird the pilot stepped on the left rudder pedal, increasing the pitch of the tail rotor-blades and making the aircraft swing left to come up behind the creature. Shaking his head, Taylor said, "I hope you guys know what you're doing because I sure as hell don't." His brown face was lightly basted with sweat. He moved the control column forward and asked, "How fast can this bird go?"

"Sixty, seventy miles an hour," Antonia said.

"Good. This baby can do two hundred."

"But it might be able to outmaneuver us—"

"Not if I can help it."

The craft now was about two hundred yards away from the eagle, which gave no sign of noticing the pursuit. The copter maintained equal speed with the bird.

Antonia looked uneasy. "She's not as large as I expected..."

"She looks pretty damn big to me," observed Taylor. "Anybody here got a game plan?"

Torino ignored the dig, his eyes fastened on the quarry. "Wingspan looks about fourteen, fifteen feet, Antonia."

"Yes, large but not abnormally so."

"If she zigzags between buildings or other structures, we'll never be able to keep up with her and we'll risk crashing," Torino said. "Force her out into open space where I can get a bead on her." He picked up the tranquilizer gun, leaving the shotgun on the seat.

Antonia looked at him. "Use the shotgun if you have to, David."

He nodded. She was going against her instincts and training and he respected it. "Tell me, if I manage to fire the sedative into her won't the fall to the ground kill her?"

"The drug should take effect slowly. As she feels herself weakening she'll probably fly to a perch somewhere before losing consciousness."

Taylor spoke up. "I hate to be a killjoy, but I figure we got about twenty minutes of fuel left."

"We'll just have to work fast," Torino said.

But his voice lacked conviction.

Antonia watched the eagle as it flew ahead of them. "The golden eagle is *very* territorial. She'll fight to protect her range even against members of her own species. She adopts an immediate flight-attack pattern to ward off intruders of all sorts—other birds, light aircraft . . . "

"You mean she might attack the copter? Like a kamikaze mission?" Torino said.

"Could be," said Antonia, face tight.

Taylor now looked worried. "We don't want her getting tangled up in the rudder. Torque will spin this machine around like crazy. We could crash . . . "

Torino looked at Antonia. As an ex-pilot he was accustomed to aeronautic danger, at least the idea of it. He wondered about her, a civilian, after all. Her expression, however, showed less fear than determination. Someone might have said the lady had the right stuff.

"I'll pull up beside her and hover," Taylor said.

The helicopter came abreast of the bird. The raptor, head tilted now toward the pursuers, fixed them with an unblinking glare. Then, without warning, the eagle pinwheeled toward earth.

Taylor depressed the pitch lever and the aircraft plunged downward in hot pursuit. The bird glided low over water, riding the thermals of the bay, heading toward the Brooklyn shoreline. The helicopter hovered above, silhouetted by the setting sun. It would be dark even before they ran out of fuel.

Torino shouldered the tranquilizer gun.

"Wait until she's over land," Antonia said. "We don't want her to drown."

Taylor grimaced over the instrument panel. "Hey, I can't swim either, lady."

The eagle flapped wings, pitching north toward the bridge.

The copter followed. Suddenly the bird dove and glided under the structure. The bridge's suspension cables loomed before the windshield. Taylor raised the lever and the helicopter climbed steeply, narrowly missing the top of the bridge. As they reached the other side of the Verrazano, Torino searched the darkening sky. "Where the hell'd she go?"

"Hell's the right place for her," said Taylor, gripping the control column.

"*There*," said Antonia, pointing upward.

The eagle was climbing, wheeling in majestic spirals toward the emerging stars.

"Hold on," Taylor said, flying the chopper first backward, then climbing after the elusive predator. Just as the helicopter was narrowing the gap the creature suddenly glided and shifted course.

The thing was headed straight toward them.

"What the devil..." muttered Taylor.

"She's in a combat pattern," Antonia said.

"What'll she do?" asked Torino.

"Don't wait to find out," said Taylor. "With all due respect, lieutenant, blast her with the shotgun."

Torino saw the signs of conflict in Antonia's face.

"Use it if you have to, David."

At first it seemed the oncoming raptor would destroy herself, but now the bird pulled up sharply, hovering on the air currents over the streets of Bay Ridge, then circled the aircraft.

"She's probably looking for a weak spot in this big bird's armor," said Antonia.

"She hits our tail rotor, we're in big trouble," Taylor came back at her.

Torino leaned out of the helicopter door, his face stung by the blast of cold air. He calculated they had about five, six minutes before darkness and fifteen minutes of fuel left.

He tried to aim the tranquilizer but the shuddering of the craft in the hover pattern made it hard to keep the gun steady.

He tried to call up the sharpshooting techniques drilled into him in both military and police training, but they eluded him in the biting air over Brooklyn. Actually he had never fired a gun in his life except at a target on the firing range to fulfill police regs.

He aimed. He fired. He missed.

Suddenly the helicopter shook as the raptor slammed into the machine's side. Torino had lost his footing and pitched forward. Taylor, somehow, got the copter back on an even keel, and the three of them scanned the sky.

It was Antonia who spotted the raptor flying south toward the tinker-toy skyline of Coney Island.

Taylor now quickly closed the distance between machine and bird. Within thirty seconds the raptor had glided into another turn—headed straight toward them.

Over the loud chatter of the rotors the pilot yelled, "She's pointed right at my goddamn tail. Shoot the son of a bitch, lieutenant."

Torino looked at the shotgun, then at Antonia.

She nodded.

Torino quickly put down the tranquilizer gun and picked up the shotgun.

The bird spread its fantail and braked, talons poised over the copter's rudder. In a moment seemingly frozen out of time, Torino took aim.

But did not fire. "I'm afraid I'll hit our own tail, she's too close . . ."

Taylor, having tilted the control column to the side, avoided by a hair a collision between the eagle and tail rotor. He knew Torino was right.

It was almost dark. The eagle fled again. In a minute

pursuers and pursued approached the canyons of downtown Manhattan, where the bird used its superior maneuverability to elude the helicopter. Time and again Torino shouldered the shotgun only to have to put it down out of fear he'd hit the windows of a skyscraper.

"How much fuel?" he asked Taylor.

"Five minutes."

"Don't you have a reserve tank?"

"About five more minutes, but we need that to find a place to land."

Darkness had now gathered over the city, but they still had the eagle in sight. "Okay," said Torino, "let's give it one more try."

The eagle flew west, the copter still in pursuit. Abruptly the south tower of the World Trade Center appeared in the windshield, a mountain of steel.

Taylor's eyes widened as he shifted the control column, just avoiding the building.

The eagle banked toward Brooklyn again. The copter caught up with her over open space. Torino hefted the shotgun again. Now he had her. He shouldered the gun, squinted. When she was about ten feet from the copter he focused, and slowly squeezed the trigger. The weapon jolted against his body. He missed again. Goddam eyes...

Antonia had been busy too. She had picked up the tranquilizer gun, waited for Torino to fire the lethal round, then fired herself.

The dart struck the bird.

The bird flew in erratic circles toward earth.

The helicopter hovered.

"Let's not lose her," said Antonia.

Taylor eyed the fuel gauge. "Let's get this baby on the ground."

Taylor depressed the lever and guided the helicopter down

to a patch of fresh budding greenery on *terra firma*, Brooklyn.

Two hours later, after an extensive search with backup help, they found the raptor in a sand trap on Dyker Beach Golf Course just outside the Fort Hamilton Military Reservation. Inspecting with a flashlight, Antonia examined the eagle, which was alive but seriously injured. The dart had entered the body in the back between the scapulars and mantle. It had been injured in its combat with the helicopter and, apparently, in the fall to the ground. While Antonia and Parks Department assistants took charge of the injured bird, Torino notified Chief Piccolo, who called Commissioner Duren, who called Bannister with the news.

Mayor Santiago was delighted.

"Call up all your news monkey pals," he told Bannister. "I want it on the eleven o'clock shows and the first editions."

"What about your earlier denials?"

"So what? They can't argue with success."

Santiago reflected for a moment, then added, "Well, the coast is clear for the visit by the Paris delegation. You ready for them, Joe?"

"Yes, we're in good shape, unless something else goes wrong."

THE eleven o'clock broadcasts and morning papers trumpeted the news. Daybreak joggers reappeared on the trails of Central Park and Riverside Park. Hikers resumed walking the nature trails of Alley Pond Park in Queens. Picnickers braving the gusts of March spread blankets again on the rolling terrain of Clove Lakes Park in Staten Island at twilight. Horseback riders emerged on the bridle paths of Pelham Parkway in the Bronx. Anglers at dawn cast lines off bridges in the Flatlands of Brooklyn.

Antonia, who had gotten permission from the federal authorities to take the raptor into her custody, placed it in a large cage in her terrace greenhouse, where she intended to try to nurse the bird back to health and conduct biological studies. The police had offered protection but she turned it down. The cage was strong enough to hold the bird under any circumstances. And having guards around would disrupt her personal life, she said.

In her preliminary examinations of the eagle she noted again that it was not as large as the testimony of Hannah Bright and other indications had led her to expect. Moreover, the bird wore no jesses and bells. Of course, they might have fallen off...

Antonia did not share the euphoria of the rest of the city. She felt uneasy, profoundly uneasy.

Twenty-three

GEORGE EGRI WIPED his bloody hands on the garishly mottled white apron and looked up at the sky. The night shift at the Gansevoort Market was nearly over, he noted with relief. He could tell by the daubs of pastel color that seeped into the horizon. George walked slowly along Gansevoort Street toward West Street. "Waddled" would be a better word. George was fat, as a butcher should be, but George was not cold-blooded, as butchers were reputed to be. In the cold dawn he felt sympathy for the—the *person* he was expecting to meet in a few minutes. He often wished there were something he could do to erase the anguish the child must feel, living the way she did. Why did he use the feminine pronoun? He knew that the youngster had been born a member of the male sex. He could tell from the way the adam's apple bobbed in her beardless throat under layers of makeup when she spoke. Still, she seemed to George to have an essential femininity that went beyond the outward

signs of her transvestism. Something in her character rebelled at having been endowed with male genitalia and
being imprisoned in the body of an alien gender. George
was very fond of her. She had a quality of sweet vulnerability
that he always had prized in the women he had known. The
very few women. He was not ashamed to admit to himself
how relatively inexperienced he was in dealings with
women, especially in sexual matters. So what? Was inno-
cence a crime? Were his long droughts of chastity something
to be ashamed of? He leaped over a puddle of blood in the
street.

In fact, he reflected, the person he was meeting reminded
him very much of his first female friend, whom he had
known in the chattering wheat fields east of the Danube so
long ago. He parted the mists of memory. He was stunned
that he could still recall her name—Maria Theresa. It was
in his birthplace, Rakamaz near Tokaj. The fields shim-
mered with grain, corn, potatoes, turnips. The hillsides
dripped with the sweet golden grapes from which oozed
without artificial pressure the rare and fine imperial Tokay
wine. He smiled to himself at the parallel that just occurred
to him: his own sweet basket of grapes also now felt over-
ripe, bursting with juice. Was it not coincidental that both
Maria Theresa and the child of the streets bestowed the
same intimate favor on him?

Maria Theresa had died in the war that accompanied the
repulsion of the Germans by the Soviets. Maybe the child
on West Street was her reincarnation, a peasant girl of Hun-
gary trapped in the flesh of a man. What an idea! It was not
so strange to believe this. Not if, like George Egri, one had
a trace of Gypsy blood.

Of course money changed hands in his dealings with the
child. But this, he believed, didn't cheapen the connection.
She was obviously in desperate need of money. Ten dollars.
It was all that George could afford on a regular basis, and

the child accepted it without protest, never hinting in any way that it was not a fair amount. Maybe the clockwork regularity of their meetings compensated for the smallness of the sum. Or maybe it was a generous amount. George Egri really did not know.

He wished he could give her more. He considered the relationship based on friendship and affection. It was not a cold business transaction. Yes, he wished he could afford to give her more.

Sometimes, though, he worried about the true nature of his motives. He had no homosexual inclinations, he was confident of this. Indeed, it was the girl-boy's extreme femininity that attracted him. But wasn't there a vein of exploitation here? This idea troubled him as he trudged over the cobblestones. He had been meeting her almost every work night for two months. It was getting to be an obsession, this ten-minute tryst in the playground across the street from the Department of Sanitation dock on pier fifty-three. He often thought about her over the weekend too. They exchanged few words, hardly looked at each other most of the time. Yet George felt a bond forming between them. Was it self-delusion? He hoped not. George had no family or even distant relatives. He kept three cats in his Queens apartment. George really had no one in his life, no one but this child whose name he didn't even know.

A brilliant gilded day was dawning over the Hudson as George walked along absorbed in such thoughts. The pale western sky was scattered with little lustrous clouds now just becoming visible. Day was breaking earlier now. The butcher quickened his pace. From their infrequent verbal exchanges he had gleaned a few facts about her life. She was a runaway from a city somewhere upstate. She was part Puerto Rican and had prominent cheekbones that reminded him of Magyar. The yellow of her hair came out of a bottle. She was, of course, addicted to drugs, crack probably, al-

172

though he didn't know for certain. George sometimes worried about getting AIDS from her but he didn't think about this very much. He had read up on the subject. He found out that it was rare for the male partner to get the disease unless they somehow exchanged blood. He inspected himself regularly. He expected that he was fairly safe. In any case, he reasoned, nothing was absolutely safe in this life and working on the night shift of the Gansevoort Meat Market was in itself a risky business, wasn't it? Moreover, living in New York didn't exactly qualify one for a low-premium life insurance policy. All things considered, he was not strong-willed enough to sever the connection anyhow. He concluded that he would rather risk a vague death than have nothing but the clear reality of slopping milk to cats and butchering animals for the steel hook. He strongly needed these nightly encounters stolen from the routines of reality.

Out of habit he looked both ways before crossing Washington Street, although it was too early for much traffic. Across the river he could see the crestfallen slips and piers of Hoboken. He entered the park, heading for the abandoned brick building in its center that in a more innocent era had been labeled a "comfort station." There she usually waited for him.

He stopped in his tracks, ears tingling. Nervously, he again wiped his hands on his blood-spattered clothes. At this hour there were none of the usual city noises to mute the sound.

The sound of bells.

George Egri looked all around him. He saw nothing unusual. He saw nothing unusual because he did not look up.

Not until it was too late.

GANYMEDE

Twenty-four

RAVEN LOKKA, IN a grim mood, drove the land rover back from town at a high speed. His weathered face, a face rutted with signs of premature aging, did not betray the excitement he felt or the adrenalin that coursed through his body. His hands perspired on the steering wheel, his mind careened with thoughts, plans.

He entered the house and threw the newspaper down on the round oak dining table under the cut-glass lamp. He put on a Bach fugue and poured himself a little whiskey before sitting down to read again the article under the New York City dateline.

Not a trace of doubt about it. It was Brunhild.

The liquor bit his tongue as his thoughts backtracked over all the years. How much time had passed? Eight years? Time that had blunted the torment to a dull but distant ache. Slowly now the wound reopened.

It was she.

Brunhild, sister of Attila, rival of Gudrun, bird of prey. Lokka sat drinking whiskey, and thirsting for revenge.

Through the window he glimpsed the cold waters of Lake Superior. Spring came late to north Minnesota and had a short life. But it was already spring in New York, he figured. He drained the whiskey glass, wondering how he had kept from going crazy. What staggering arrogance he had shown when he thought he could understand the language of birds. This arrogance, he was convinced, was what had doomed his infant son.

And later his wife.

The falconer glanced around the room, at the cast-iron stove and patch-quilt coverlets, at the driftwood sculptures and neat little seascapes in varnished frames. The home-spun sights kindled a flame of pain as he communed with the ghosts of Iris and little Jack. As long as they went un-avenged none of them would rest. With their deaths had dissolved hope of ever having a home and family. He knew that he had deserted them the very day he decided to enter the cult of falconry. Well, now he was an ordained priest of vengeance.

There was no time to waste.

He phoned Duluth Airport and reserved a seat on a North-west Airline flight leaving at 6:55 P.M. for New York via Minneapolis–St. Paul. On the scratch pad magnetized to the refrigerator he noted the flight numbers, 2652 and 745, the fare, $388, and the estimated time of arrival at La-Guardia Airport, one minute before midnight.

As he gave the ticket agent his credit card number over the phone he fretted over whether he would be able to locate a hotel room or any place to stay on such short notice. He had no relatives or friends in New York, at least not that he remembered. He had broken off all friendships since the tragedies of his infant son and then his wife. Not that he ever had a flock of friends.

He took some clothes and personal items out of drawers, closets, and cabinets and stuffed them into a duffle bag. He forced himself to stop and think. Would he need anything special? No, the police would supply peripheral things. The necessities he always carried with him—in his braincase and his hands. On impulse he went over to a drawer in his bedroom and took out the *kukri*, a knife he had picked up in the Orient, and put it in the bag.

He wondered if he should inform the authorities beforehand of his coming and his intentions. He decided not to, figuring that they might try to stop him or consider him a crank. He thought that he had a better chance of persuading them about the truth of his story in person. If they gave him a chance to show his skill at falconry he was pretty sure that would clinch it. In any case, he had no choice. He had to take this chance for vengeance.

He crammed his sleeping bag in the duffle bag, in case he had to join the ranks of New York's homeless. It didn't matter where he slept, what he ate. Where was little Jack sleeping now, so long after he was carried off by the great bird? And Iris? What ashes did she taste in the places where suicides wandered?

Soon, soon, he would give them relief. And himself.

He loaded the duffle bag in the back of the land rover and started on the lakeside route from Taconite Harbor to Duluth. Banks of snow were still piled on the roadside. Hawks wheeled in the gray sky as he turned off the service road at the junction of Route 611. Soon the road wound past Beaver Bay. He tried not to think about Iris and how he had ignored her warnings. She had never recovered from the loss of her child, descending into a psychic hell of four months before killing herself by staging an imaginary cocktail party in the tool shed and drinking a tall glass of paint thinner labeled "mineral spirits" garnished with a cocktail cherry.

She had suffered an excruciating death.

He drove on, making his mind a blank. In time he approached Two Harbors and saw the first road signs indicating the ports of Duluth and Superior in Wisconsin. He wished again that he had taken Iris' advice and given up falconry before it was too late. How many times in the past had his mind played with this pointless wish? How many times in the future would he torture himself with it? If he had a future.

Why hadn't he joined Iris? he thought as he drove into the airport parking lot. He knew the answer... because he had a rendezvous to keep. A rendezvous with the raptor.

The plane arrived in New York's LaGuardia Airport twenty-five minutes late. After picking up his duffle bag from baggage claim he consulted the newspaper clipping to check her name. Antonia Meadows. He decided that it was too late to call her now. He would do so first thing in the morning. He looked around for a tourist information desk. It was closed. He buttonholed a skycap, who directed him to a motor lodge within walking distance. He didn't really give a damn.

Joe Bannister finished reading the memo from the Medical Examiner's Office on the death of a butcher named George Egri. He looked at Antonia Meadows, who was sitting across the desk from him.

He got up and paced around his office in the west wing of City Hall. He shook his head slowly. "*Damn* it," he said under his breath. "And here we thought this thing was over. Santiago's climbing the walls."

"He's better off than George Egri."

"Yeah, right. But what do I tell the press? They've been after me nonstop for the last two days."

"Try the truth, Joe. We can't hide from it. Tell them she's still out there but we're doing everything we can to—"

"What about the eagle you and Torino did get? Don't tell me we've got a flock of them nesting in New York."

"No, I don't think so. But I suspected something was wrong right after we caught the bird and I examined him."

"*Him?*"

"Yes. The one we caught is a male. I think he could be the raptor's mate. Eagles mate for life, they're very faithful to each other. He wasn't very large either, normal-sized for a male. Not gigantic like Hannah Bright described the bird who attacked her. Of course her mind might have been playing tricks with her but I don't think so."

"Females grow bigger than males?"

"Usually, yes. I believe our raptor is an abnormally large bird. A genetic freak of some sort." She got up and walked over to the window that overlooked City Hall Park. "Hannah Bright. The wino in Central Park. Both of them described her as a giant bird. And the butcher George Egri was a powerful man. I think he would have been able to fight off a bird of ordinary size."

"Well, I hope you're wrong."

"Me too." But she was almost certain she wasn't.

A beeping sound came from her purse that had been deposited on the carpeted floor. "Can I use your phone to call the office?"

"Sure."

She reached Fillipina Lopez. "Some character called *Raven Lokka* called. Said he's a falconer who can help you catch the eagle. I told him you'd get back to him but he wouldn't leave a number, said he was coming right over to wait for you. I thought you'd want to know. Sounds like a real nut job."

She might have known that the media coverage would

bring them out of the woodwork. "Maybe you'd better alert security," Antonia said. "Anybody else call?"

"Marburg. And Lieutenant Torino."

"Did he leave a number?"

"He's in his office at police headquarters."

Antonia jotted down the number, thought about calling him from Joe's phone but decided against it. "Did Marburg say what he wanted?"

"No," Fillipina said.

Antonia decided that the boss probably was just keeping tabs on her. She got out of there and headed for Broadway and the BMT subway.

BANNISTER put aside the M.E.'s memo. Everything was going fine until that fat butcher got turned into birdseed two days ago. What a nightmare. The French delegation was due to arrive in a few days. He picked up the Medical Examiner's report and headed down the hall to Santiago's office.

AT the anteroom to her office Antonia stopped at Fillipina's desk for her messages. The assistant motioned toward a man standing a few paces away studying one of the Audubon prints. "It's the man I told you about. Raven Lokka," Fillipina said. "Should I call a security guard?"

Antonia turned and inspected the man more closely. He was tall and athletic-looking, with a leathery brown, rather cadaverous face dominated by dark gray eyes. His grayish hair was long and somewhat shaggy. He wore a green fatigue jacket and corduroy pants. Although unusual looking, he did not appear crazy. She told Fillipina to forget security. Show him in.

Raven Lokka, standing now in front of Antonia, his rough-

cast face expressionless, at once fascinated and faintly re-
pelled her.

He sat in the green plastic basket chair near her desk. No
words were wasted. "I've come to help capture and destroy
the berkute."

She got up from behind the desk and walked slowly over
to a side table, where she poured herself a cup of coffee.
"How do you know it's a berkute?"

"I know Brunhild. She's an old friend—and enemy of
mine."

"Brunhild?"

"I named her. I took her as an eyass from Central Asia
and trained her to the lure." And he then told her the whole
story, from his training in falconry by Ali Kanat to the aerial
kidnapping of his child and his wife's suicide. He recounted
it all in an oddly emotionless and, to Antonia's ears, a fright-
eningly convincing way. Still, she had to test him.

"Why should I believe such a tale?"

"Because it's true."

She sipped coffee. "This could easily be some other bird."

He shook his head. "No. It's Brunhild. There is no doubt
about it."

"How can you be so sure?"

"For one thing, her size. The newspapers quoted eye-
witnesses that said she had nearly a twelve-foot wingspan.
You are a biologist, it said. You know how abnormal that
is. As a juvenile Brunhild had a ten-foot span. It's Brunhild."

Antonia, though all but persuaded, believed she had to
challenge him. "How do you know it's not another over-
sized bird? After all, the world is full of inexplicable—"

"I know it."

"What made her so large?"

"You're the scientist, please tell me."

He was reversing things, but she had to go along. "Well,

gigantism is usually caused by some glandular disturbance. In humans abnormal size most often is caused by oversecretion of growth hormones by cells in the pituitary gland. Sometimes oversecretion of the thyroid hormone also plays a part. Anyway, it results in the metabolic rate working overtime. At least twenty percent above normal. Giant humans don't live very long, though."

"How about other species?"

"I'm not sure, but I believe the same general principles apply. Abnormal growth of the long bones. Lack of secretion of growth hormones also occurs. Of course, this results in dwarfism."

"Yes, but what triggers such disturbances in the pituitary gland? Like most scientists, you say the same thing in different ways."

"Nobody knows for sure. In some way it's hereditary. Of course, normal parents produce giant and dwarf children. And vice-versa. It's really a mystery." She looked out the window. "Everything's a mystery. Each answer that we make unlocks a new question. But we're getting afield."

"Yes, but it's correct to say that gigantism is caused by a genetic disturbance of some sort?"

"Yes."

"Okay. Let's tackle the new question that *this* answer unlocks. Can a genetic defect be caused not by parental inheritance but by some external force?"

"You mean radiation, don't you?"

"It's been well-documented—hasn't it?—that electromagnetic radiation causes mutation of the genetic material of a cell."

"That's right."

"So radiation might cause alteration in the acidophilic cells of the pituitary gland?"

"Very reasonable." She was impressed. "I see you've boned up on the subject. What exactly are you driving at?"

Raven Lokka's smile was a sour one. "I have a theory about Brunhild. I believe that when she was conceived the mating place of her parents and the eyrie of Kirghizia where they brooded was corrupted by poison winds."

"I'm not sure I follow you..."

"Brunhild was born around June 10, 1986. You're an ornithologist. About how long before that was she conceived?"

"Forty, maybe forty-five days."

"Near the beginning of May."

"About then."

"Do you remember a disaster that occurred on April 25, 1986?"

She looked confused.

"In the Soviet Union. Something involving radiation."

Now she caught his meaning. "Of course. The nuclear accident at Chernobyl. But the Ukraine is hundreds of miles from Kirghizia."

"So is Lapland, where radioactive particles were carried by the winds and countless reindeer were destroyed. They found traces of radiation as far away as Japan. Like the birds, the wind doesn't respect international boundaries."

"The federal people want us to try to capture the eagle alive if possible."

"I doubt if it will be possible," he said.

"Do you have a falconer's license in Minnesota?"

"No."

"You could go to jail."

"Only if you report me. We don't need to tell the authorities that I continued practicing falconry after leaving the Soviet Union. I don't believe we have any alternative— eventually the raptor must be destroyed."

Twenty-five

When Joe Bannister arrived at Antonia's apartment, he found two other men on hand—one Torino, whom she'd called, and the other a strange fellow by the stranger name of Raven Lokka.

"A falconer? An unusual hobby," Bannister was saying to Lokka.

Lokka nodded.

"Well, sir," Bannister went on, "what makes you think you can net this monster? She's been pretty damn elusive so far."

Lokka obviously did not much like Joe Bannister. Finally he said, "I learned my craft from a teacher in Central Asia. I know the berkute's ways, especially *this* one. I also have strong personal reasons for wanting to get her. I'm willing to try. What have you got to lose?"

Bannister looked at Antonia. "He knows the eagle personally?"

186

"He thinks so. Look," she finally said, "we've promised Mr. Lokka to keep certain facts about his history confidential. Let's just say he thinks the raptor is an abnormally large berkute that fled captivity about four years ago. Well, not exactly captivity but the control of a falconer."

"Who promised confidentiality?" Bannister asked.

"David and I."

"This is an evil bird," Lokka said in a chillingly quiet voice.

Bannister took a big sip of his drink. This character was a candidate for Bellevue, but what the hell, he was willing to try anything to get rid of "the winged menace," as the tabloids had called it.

"Lokka thinks we might be able to hand-trap the bird," Antonia was saying.

"It's worth a try," Lokka said. "A trick I learned in Central Asia. The berkute is fairly helpless if you disarm the talons in a hand-trap. At least it works with normal eagles."

"But this one's abnormal," Bannister said.

"What about her beak?" asked Torino.

"Not as lethal as the talons," Lokka said. "I'll wear a fencing mask and thick leather clothing. She's very strong but I might be able to handle her."

"How will you find her?" Bannister asked.

"Flush her out of hiding with a lure. She's been trained to the lure."

"The Sheep Meadow in Central Park," said Antonia. "It's near the zoo, where she's made a strike before and where she was seen bathing in the fountain. She seems attracted to the place; it's the closest thing to a wilderness in the middle of the city."

Bannister looked doubtful. "Seems like a long shot. I think you said this bird has a range of over a hundred miles."

"I'll call to her," said Lokka. "In her earliest, formative

years she was trained to answer the falconer's call. She will remember it."

"We'll do it at dawn," said Antonia. "We'll get the police to block off traffic and keep people out. We may have to try the whole operation a few times before it works—"

"It might leak to the press," said Bannister.

"We'll have to chance that," Torino said.

Bannister turned to Antonia. "How's the bird's boy friend doing?"

"Poorly. Refuses to eat."

"Think it will die?"

"I hope not."

Bannister looked at Lokka, whose grim expression seemed carved in his face. "What do you use as a lure?"

"Normally the hawker uses something like a piece of fur with beefsteak or fresh-killed rabbit tied to it. But there are more effective ways. I studied the German falconer Jaeger. He trained in Central Asia, like I did. He trained berkutes to kill wolves by turning them loose on children—"

"*Children?*" said Bannister.

"Children impersonating wolves. Covered with protective leather and wolfskin with raw meat tied to their backs. Once the berkutes struck against the children, they would be ready to strike against wolves, their main prey."

Torino broke in: "*You* don't propose to use kids, do you?"

"No. But I do intend to use a person clothed in wolfskin. Brunhild was trained in this manner and it will increase our chances of flushing her out."

"Brunhild?" said Bannister.

"The name he gave her," Antonia said.

Bannister turned to the falconer. "In other words, you propose to use a human as bait?"

"Yes."

Bannister scanned the faces in the group. "Who?"

A moment's silence.

Torino slowly raised his hand. "Me," he said. And wondered if he'd taken leave of his senses.

ANTONIA lay wide awake, gave up trying to sleep, got out of bed and went over to sit in the rocking chair near the window that connected to the greenhouse. From this vantage she could see the bird cages on one side and on the other the star-sequined sky over Greenwich Village. She had rambling thoughts of David Torino, Raven Lokka and the odd predicament they all were in. She sank into a kind of limbo of consciousness between sleep and wakefulness—

Her ears tingled at the sound.

"*Cheop.*" A thin, high-pitched sound. It had come from the greenhouse. Aquilas, she knew, were usually silent, but when they did make sounds they sometimes were known to make just a thin chirp, incongruous with their large size. She had never heard an eagle's call before, but she knew from her studies that they sometimes cheeped like this and occasionally made other sounds, depending on the circumstances. For example, they were supposed to make a sharp barking sound when alarmed. They never uttered any sound without good reason.

She entered the greenhouse to investigate. The birds were asleep in their shrouded cages. She heard nothing. She went over to the eagle's cage and took the cover off. The bird cowered in the corner, spearing her with yellow eyes. She noted that he still had not touched the ground beef she'd left him in the feeder.

So why had he cheeped? Had something upset him? Excited him? She started to put the cover back on the cage.

Suddenly she heard another sound.

She could not pinpoint the source but knew it had come

from somewhere outside. She heard it faintly but ever more distinctly. Unlocking the greenhouse door, she went outside onto the terrace. She shivered in her nightgown.

The mewling sound grew louder. She looked up, and what she saw in the sky made her throat clog.

The spiraling form blotted out the crescent moon, and at the moment Antonia felt not so much afraid as spellbound by the awful beauty of this aerial ballet being performed. The eagle's great marginated wings fluttered like the immense fans of an olympian coquette as she hovered over the jagged horizon. The plaintive sound of her mewling was answered by the chirping that resumed inside the greenhouse. Now she swooped in circular patterns at the altitude of the water towers, coming closer, closer. Antonia stumbled backward. She was nearly mesmerized, afraid and unsure. Should she reach for the cordless phone under the awning? Should she look around for something to use as a weapon? She stood there, open-mouthed, immobilized as the dark form glided nearer.

Suddenly the raptor braked with her fantail, banked left and flew off into the night—apparently startled by the raucous din of an automobile alarm that had gone off in a car parked on the street directly below. Antonia's breathing began to return to normal.

She still could not quite take in the performance she had witnessed. Brunhild had been doing a courtship dance, the mewling had been her mating call.

> *The great bird of prey, a spot in the immense sky, flaps the dark shroud of her wings to increase her speed and escape the banshee wail on the street far below. She turns her cloudy eyes with their shielding nictating membranes toward the south, where tonight friendly winds originate and*

where the nest lies. She has been frightened away by the loud whine that drowned out the voice of her mate and the summons of her flesh. She is thwarted for now from following impulses surfacing from the deepest well of genetic memory. For now.

But she marks the place well.

Twenty-six

THE NEXT MORNING David Torino was badly upset when he heard about Antonia's close encounter with the killer bird. He had been tempted to advise her to have the mate stuffed and donate him to the American Museum of Natural History. Instead he suggested that the male bird be taken either to the Bronx or Central Park Zoo. Keeping the eagle in her apartment might well endanger her life, he argued for the umpteenth time.

No use. She regarded it as a chance to unlock scientific mysteries. And the danger not only did not deter her, it seemed to energize her.

"Besides," she had told the detective, "you're putting yourself in a hell of a lot more danger than I am."

"That's different..."

"Why?"

"I'm paid to take risks. It's my job."

"Risk-taking is a way of life for anyone who wants to accomplish anything in life."

She was one hardheaded lady, he thought as he hung up the phone. But wasn't that one of her attractions? He had always been turned off by women who were pushovers, with Geisha-like mentalities. He also began to think about his own tendency to take risks, such as volunteering to act as claw-bait for one of the largest birds of prey in recorded history. There were no easy answers. Part of the job? But mixed in was an old slay-the-dragon syndrome left over from a kid's fantasy. As an adult it had helped get him into the Air Force as a pilot. There was a lot of *hubris* in it, he knew, playing hero, and it did nothing to prevent the cold sweats every time he pictured what he'd committed himself to doing soon. Very soon.

RAVEN Lokka and everyone else involved felt pressed for time, so it had been decided that they would have one practice run today before going on to the real thing tomorrow at dawn. Torino took a deep breath.

The phone rang again. It was his mother.

"I saw you the other day on the tee-vee," she informed him.

"Yeah? How did I look, mom?"

He could picture her shrugging at the other end of the line.

"Not as handsome as your father, but pretty good."

"Thanks, I guess."

"That lady beside you in the news *conferenza*? She your gell fren'?"

"Not yet, sweetheart. But light a couple of candles, will you?"

"She's beautiful. But she look kinda cold."

"I think I can warm her up."

"Don't talk like that to your mother." A pause, then: "Bring her around some night."

"I'll sure try."

"When I see you, anyhow?"

"I don't know. Soon."

"You be careful, hear? When you gonna catch this big eagle?"

"We're working on it."

"You be careful."

"I will. And, mom?"

"Eh?"

"Don't go out on the terrace too much."

"What? I gotta water the plants—"

"Don't do it at dawn or dusk."

"You bet," she said quickly. Mom was no fool.

"You been making the novena?" he asked.

"Sure."

"Say a couple of prayers for me."

"I always do," she said in a dark tone of voice.

TORINO felt sheepish in wolf's clothing, even though joggers, cyclists, and other passersby in the park paid little attention to him in his getup. To New Yorkers the bizarre was commonplace. Besides feeling more than a little ridiculous he also felt hot, dressed as he was in a fencing mask, leather clothes from neck to foot and wolfskin.

Raven Lokka wore a fencing mask too, and protective clothing that included leather gloves that they hoped would be thick enough to protect his hands but flexible enough to allow maneuverability. Along with them were two plainclothes officers from headquarters.

The plan was fairly simple: Torino, disguised as the wolf, would circle around on all fours with the hunk of beefsteak tied to his back. Lokka, hiding nearby, would utter the distinctively high-pitched falconer's call that he had learned from Ali Kanat. He would be poised to leap out and hand-trap the eagle's legs when—if—she stooped to the bait. The hand-trap was a successful technique of the Plains Indians of North America who used eagle feathers for decoration, the method leaving the bird helpless to fight with the talons. If it worked.

Torino had doubts. This was an unusually powerful bird of a very powerful species. He knew that Lokka was part Indian but he doubted that he had somehow inherited the skill of his ancestors. But Lokka was willing to try, and so was Torino.

The falconer was supposed to manacle the bird before she snatched away the meat or had a chance even to try to sink her talons into the human bait. As an extra precaution the beef was to be smeared with birdlime that might stick to the eagle's head and, one hoped, temporarily blind her. The two plainclothes officers would also be standing by with a trammel net to secure her capture. Or try to.

The group spent only about two hours in the park, getting used to the gear and the routine. When they thought they had everything laid out, Lokka turned to Torino, who was drenched in sweat, and said it was time to call it quits for the day.

Torino nodded and began struggling out of the outfit.

Lokka glanced up at the westering sun. "I'll wake you up at four A.M. We'd better hit the sack early, get a good night's sleep."

Fat chance, Torino thought.

THE day dawned warm and clear. But the operation was a washout—everybody showed up but the guest of honor. She appeared to have made other plans. It was the same on the

second day, and the third. Torino felt increasingly frus-
trated, not to mention itchy as hell from having to wear
leather and animal skin. He upped his ration from two to
three scotches at the end of the day. The whole team was
beginning to lose it, except Lokka, whose patience seemed
biblical as he urged them to try again.

THE fourth morning was cold and windy with sporadic out-
breaks of misty rain. Conditions like these would interfere
with even the great eagle's fabled vision, and they considered postponing the event. But after consultations among
Lokka, Antonia, Bannister and other agents of City Hall it
was decided to go ahead as planned. What was there to lose
except one more itchy day for Torino? Bannister especially
urged them to go ahead with it. The planning calendar that
lay open on his desk showed that the World's Fair delegation
was scheduled to arrive from Paris the next day.

As usual, police crews put up barricades, closing off both
the East Drive and West Drive of the park, leaving open the
four transverse roads. News of the operation had still not
leaked to the press—a sort of miracle in itself. The operation
was centered in the Sheep Meadow, just beyond the zoo,
between the two drives and just north of Traverse Road No.
1. The area was roped off, with police officers stationed
every few yards to make sure nobody straggled in or inter-
fered. The officers themselves were told nothing about what
was going on except what was absolutely necessary.

The humidity made Torino feel even more clammy and
tense in the leather and wolfskin as he waited for dawn to
break.

The day now arrived without the usual fanfare of color,
gray light seeping gradually into the sky. Torino heard his
heart thumping.

Antonia, giving in partly to Torino and his worry about

her safety, stationed herself some twenty yards away at the old bowling green. Wearing a nautical yellow warm-up jacket and black tights, she observed through high-powered binoculars. She seemed cool as a stone in a mountain stream. Seemed.

Lokka too had argued for her to keep some distance from the scene. The fewer people around the better, he had said. The raptor had a poor sense of smell but, of course, keen eyesight. So the strategy called for keeping humans hidden from sight as much as possible. The plainclothes officers with the net concealed themselves behind a nearby tree. Lokka followed his usual procedure of covering himself with tree branches while lying in a hole in the middle of the meadow that was circled by the sham wolf.

Lokka, standing now, snuffed the air.

"Think she'll come this time? Torino asked.

"I have a feeling she will," he said flatly, his voice muffled by the fencing mask.

The sixth sense of the blood sportsman? Torino wondered.

"Let's get started."

Torino loped across the Sheep Meadow.

Lokka climbed into the hole in the ground and arranged the branches around him. He left open a space through which he could see the gauzy air. Then he cupped his mouth and gave out the falconer's call.

Fog mantles the man-made peaks of the city as the raptor flies. She hears the call again, over time, over space. The familiar call that sparks in the electric field of her brain visions of wolves, memories of blood. The air she flies on is full of mist but her consciousness is crystal clear. She can't resist any longer. She remembers the man from the time of earliest light. She flies toward the sound that comes from the big newly green place. The place of water and prey.

Torino, the prey, continued to circle the meadow on all fours, feeling foolish, tired and scared. He had been going through the routine for only twenty minutes or so but it felt like at least an hour. Every so often he heard Lokka's eerie birdcall. He would play the wolf under the slate sky, but he increasingly felt it was for nothing—

He heard the bells.

His body stiffened.

He heard a thunderous wingbeat.

Trailing jesses, the eagle dropped like a stone on the prey.

Through the protective covering, in the split second before she slammed into him, Torino caught a glimpse of the plummeting raptor. If he lived to have grandchildren, how would he describe her to them? The thunderbird of Nootka paintings holding the leviathan in her claws? Such an image failed miserably to convey her hideous power and grace.

Raising her hackles, unfurling her plumage, unsheathing her talons, she landed on his back. Close up was her pitiless face. *Where was Lokka?* He felt total panic as he stared straight into those veiled eyes.

Torino was sent sprawling to the damp ground. The bird mantled over him triumphantly.

Where was Lokka?

It all happened in an instant . . . A great clattering of the fan of feathers, a strange bark of fright. And the falconer had thrown himself on the raptor, trying to manacle her wrists.

Torino rolled free, regained his feet and goggled at the struggle between falconer and bird. She had spread her wings to an uncanny length and continued to bark as Lokka, muttering, sweating, wrestled with her legs and tried to hold on.

But he was not a match for the eagle, which wrested her yellow limbs free of his grasp, flapped her wings and lifted off into the rolling fog. She banked around with what actually seemed to be a glance of cold recognition at her old trainer, twitched and fluttered her wings again, caught an updraft and vanished into the turbid sky.

Lokka sat on a boulder, eyes smoldering. He slammed his fist into his gloved palm. "I had her, right here."

Torino threw off the wolfskin, shook his head in disbelief. "My God, a monster. I wouldn't have believed it. She's just too strong to capture by a hand-trap."

Antonia and the others stood by, speechless.

Lokka's hands now fell limply to his sides.

"Just too strong," Torino muttered again.

Lokka did not say anything as he gazed at the opaque sky, which to him seemed to represent an affronting universe. His mouth was clamped shut. He seemed to be funneling his long held grief and anger into one deep pool of hatred.

Twenty-seven

TORINO SAT WITH Guy on the carpeted floor of the boy's bedroom helping him assemble a Lego siege tower from a puzzling array of interlocking plastic pieces. Nanook was sprawled on the carpet, muzzle on paws, regarding them with blank moist eyes.

Torino was finding it hard to concentrate; he kept thinking about his terrifying encounter with the raptor and the likelihood that he soon would get a second chance at more of the same. He also thought about Raven Lokka's reaction to the failure to hand-trap the creature. Lokka agreed that she was now too big and strong to trap by conventional methods. He had argued to the Mayor and anybody who would listen that they should not risk human life any more and just destroy her. *If* they could find her again. Torino had noticed how hollow-eyed the falconer was, and after some probing learned that Lokka, whose motel room was under the flight path of a jumbo jet a minute, had not been sleeping. He handed Lokka the keys to his apartment and convinced him to stay with him.

It was Mary's night off and Torino had volunteered to sit with Guy for a couple of hours while Antonia tried nursing the ailing male eagle in the greenhouse. He also, of course, welcomed the chance to be around her. Bannister was out of the way, squiring members of the French group around town. The press secretary was relieved that for the time being, at least, the newspapers had been downplaying the eagle story, focusing instead on an apparently racially motivated slaying of a Pakistani cab driver on Staten Island. New Yorkers, case-hardened by a staple diet of crime and violence, had short attention spans. So while Bannister's public relations problem was by no means solved, the edge had been blunted some by the passing of a few days.

Until, unless disaster struck again, Torino thought.

As if to punctuate that thought, Antonia now burst into the room, her face flushed.

"What's wrong?" he asked.

"The eagle's dead," she said.

JOE Bannister wore a freeze-dried smile as he and the four Parisians stood in the blue-carpeted lobby of the World Trade Center Tower Number Two, waiting for an express elevator to whisk them nonstop to the glass-enclosed observation deck that stood suspended on a steel skeleton nearly a quarter of a mile up in the sky. The group was composed of three middle-aged men and one woman, a fortyish strawberry blonde with a trim figure who did little to camouflage her interest in Bannister. What the hell, he thought, it might come in handy during negotiations over the World's Fair site selection.

As the elevator shuddered up to the 107th floor he glanced at his watch, noting that they were on schedule. He had planned to arrive at the observatory just about a half-hour before dusk to give them the full impact of the view during both daylight and the shimmering electrically lit night. He had already escorted them to Chinatown, Little Italy, the South Street Seaport and the World Financial Center. Tonight they would dine across the Brooklyn Bridge at the River Café.

The elevator came to a stop and they emerged on the observatory some 1,310 feet above sea level. It had been a fairly clear day although a horde of dark clouds could be seen amassing in the west over New Jersey, providing the descending sun a palette on which to splash rosy color. The sights before them in all directions were identified by stenciling on the windows. Bannister also prompted the delegates as they moved from east to south, taking in views of the Verrazano-Narrows Bridge, the parachute jump at Coney Island and the Brooklyn and Manhattan bridges—the great cyclorama of the city. When they came to the windows that faced north Bannister began pointing out landmark skyscrapers, including the RCA and Chrysler buildings, Empire State Building, Metropolitan Life Tower and, almost directly below, that Gothic gem, the Woolworth Building. As they took in the sights Bannister told them the story of their countryman Phillipe Petit, who in 1974 walked on a high wire between the two towers of the World Trade Center. "He even got down on one knee and bowed to the crowd," Bannister said. "I covered it for a local television station."

"*Est fou*," said the woman, Madame Blanche DeVoto.

"Did he say why he tried such a stunt?" another delegate asked.

"He made some comment about how if he saw oranges he had to juggle them and if he saw tall towers he had to walk between them."

"I remember," said the delegate. "He did the same thing between the towers of Notre Dame."

"I suppose living dangerously can be exhilarating," said Madame DeVoto, pressing her hip against Bannister's.

He quickly suggested, "Why don't we go up to the outdoor observation deck? We can see Flushing Meadows from there."

Outside the sky was taking on a glowering aspect as the storm and night came nearer. "Very dramatic," said Madame DeVoto, huddling into the collar of her brown suede jacket. Bannister and she stood on the north end of the deck while the other delegates wandered about.

He walked over to a set of coin-operated binoculars and put quarters in the slot. "Would you care to look through these?"

"I prefer the view from here," she said.

He tried to acknowledge the come-on without encouraging it. And promptly thought of Antonia, and how upset she had been when he had talked to her this morning about the death of the eagle. She seemed to take it as some kind of personal failure. She also seemed to regard it as some undefined evil omen, which was hardly her style. In any case, it had put her into a dark mood.

He again urged the French woman to use the binoculars. She shrugged and did so. After looking around for a while she removed her eyes from the machine and, pointing to the northeast, asked, "What's the beautiful building right there? The one with the marvelous spires and stone traceries?"

"The Woolworth Building," he said, pleased at the diversion and grateful that he had boned up on such landmark buildings' history. "The Cathedral of Commerce, somebody called it. Let's see, built by Frank Woolworth, the five-and-dime king, in 1913. It was the tallest building in the world until the Empire State Building went up. In fact, except for your own Eiffel Tower, it was the tallest structure in the world."

She gave him a smile. "I love skyscrapers. Big and pointy."

He tried to ignore the obvious. "Yes, well, it cost thirteen-and-a-half million dollars, all of it paid in cash."

"Did Mr. Woolworth pay for it in nickels and dimes?" she asked.

"No doubt." He inserted more coins and she peered again through the binoculars.

"I see there is an observation gallery, too."

"Yes. But it's been closed for many years." He glanced idly in the opposite direction, where the sun was sinking into a cushion of clouds.

"*Holá*," the woman suddenly shouted. "What is *that*?" She continued to peer through the binoculars.

"What is what?"

"Some large shadow in the tower of the Woolworth Building." She swiveled the machine toward him. "Here. Look for yourself."

He gripped the knobs on the side of the instrument, adjusted the focus and looked. The waning sunlight gilded the final of the green copper tower. He let his eyes trace downward.

Now far away from the seaport she flies on up-drafts of wind some 790 feet above the pavements of Broadway. Shadows lengthen below the soaring Asian queen of eagles whose far-seeing eyes reflect the slanting rays of the sun. She is magnetized by the white-brick building where she last heard her mate's call somewhere in the cliffs and gullies of Greenwich Village. She is compelled by an ineffable instinct toward the place. She turns up her

204

*wingtips under the air pressure, rotates her gilded
head from side to side. What does she know? What
does she hear? No owl of ill omen hoots to her.
She hears nothing but silence. She clicks her beak
and squarks, a raw and bristling sound.*

GUY was playing with the stuffed teddy bear on the carpeted
floor of the living room near the sneakered feet of Mary,
who sat in an armchair reading a bodice-ripper.

The little boy looked up at her. "Homer and I want Nestlé's Quik. Can we have some, please?"

She got up, putting the book down on an end table. "Okay,
okay." She headed for the kitchen, turned to say, "Then
you and Homer have to start getting ready for bed. Hear
me?"

She entered the kitchen, leaving the boy sitting near the
french doors leading to the terrace. The doors, slightly ajar,
allowed a breeze to filter in. The sky outside looked omi-
nous, portending rain.

When Mary got to the kitchen the phone rang. She picked
up the receiver of a console mounted on the wall. "Oh, *hi*,
Carlo," she said in a sugary voice. It was the boy she had
met Saturday night, the one with the sweet smile and beautiful long poker-straight hair. It wasn't long before she was
deep in conversation with Carlo.

Back in the living room the boy informed the teddy bear
of the upcoming treat. Nanook, sprawled nearby with his
muzzle on his paws, suddenly stirred. The dog's ears stiffened. He stared out the window at the mottled sky, brushed
with ever-darkening hues. The dog scrambled to his feet
and panted, then padded over to the terrace door and began
to whimper.

"I think Nanook wants some Nestlé's Quik too," Guy
told the stuffed animal.

TALONS

The dog brought a growl out of the abyss of his throat, then trotted out onto the terrace. He placed his paws on the armrest of a deck chair to raise himself to a position where he could scan the murky sky.

He began to howl.

Guy held the bear by one ear. "What's the matter with Nanook, Homer? Nanook's crying. Let's go see."

Cuddling the stuffed animal, the boy followed the dog out to the terrace. Nanook continued to form the rumbling sounds deep in his throat as the surrounding air suddenly was filled with the chiming of a small bell.

Twenty-eight

ANTONIA GOT UP from the bentwood chair in the Seaport pub where she was meeting with Torino to go over what had happened and what to do. "I'm going to call home to make sure Mary's got Guy off to bed."

She returned in a minute, a frown on her face. "Line's busy," she said. "That girl's ear has grown to the phone." She sipped her drink. A minute or so later she tried again. After the third try she told David she wanted to leave. "I can't get through and I'm worried. Sorry, nervous mother."

"Sure," he said. He raised his hand, motioning for the check.

She shook her head. "Don't wait for the waiter. Leave money on the table and let's just go. Right now."

He didn't question her. In a cab she sat silently staring straight ahead. He left her alone and glanced out of the taxi window. Night had gathered over the columned court-houses of Foley Square. Nothing to do or say except wait for the cab to snake through traffic toward Greenwich Village. It was the climax of the rush hour and the streets were still snarled with honking, muttering motorists. Suddenly Antonia turned her face toward him and took hold of his hand. He knew enough to say nothing as they crossed Canal Street, the traffic thinned, and the driver gunned the motor.

A few blocks away in Torino's apartment Raven Lokka was rummaging through his frayed duffle bag. As he searched, his mind teemed with jumbled memories of Kirghizia and Minnesota, of Ali Kanat and Iris and Jack. Most of all, his son Jack. He had a memory, hazy around the edges, of playing piggyback with the child. A laughing child. A sacrificial lamb. As he rummaged and remembered, his body swayed as if he were on a jerking train that was going backward. He was determined to perform the deed that would avenge the terrible loss of his son, and at least in part atone for his own persistent guilt. He knew that the stain was indelible. But only one agent would wash it even partly away—blood. The blood of a once beloved, now hated, creature.

There was no other way. He might have known: the hand-trap was a bad idea. It had been exciting to encounter Brunhild again as a mature eagle in all her fearsome power and beauty. In a perverse way he realized now that he had even *missed* her. No other way to put it.

His fingertips touched the object that he had been looking for in the duffle bag. He drew it out, sat on the couch and saw through the window the masts of restored sailing ships, gray against the darkening sky where sea gulls circled. His senses tingled. He ran a forefinger along the curved blade. His feelings were in flood tide. Thinking was idle, under the circumstances. An icy calm was not possible. But emotions were useful as an impetus to action, as an adjunct to revenge.

Wind swept in through the window, cracked open at the bottom, a wind foreshadowing a storm, the same wind the eagle used to mount into the sky. Cut flowers shivered in a vase on the coffee table. Venetian blinds chattered. The wind, bodiless ally of kites, planes, and birds. The wind that circumscribed the earth from Valparaiso to Vienna, from Nome to Nepal. Lokka had always been strangely aware of the wind, of the freedom creatures like birds had because of it. It was what had drawn him to the art of falconry, the urge to harness the wind, escape the prison of his own flesh.

He looked at the dagger. It was a *kukri* with a broad curved blade and ornamented hilt. He had gotten it in a musty shop in Katmandu that smelled of sandalwood. It was the weapon he would use . . .

THE downpour began just as they were getting out of the taxi, and David paid the driver while Antonia ran under the building canopy and through the front door held open by the doorman.

In the vestibule David stumbled over a pull toy—a wooden zebra. Antonia preceded him into the heart of the apartment, following strains of music coming from the tape deck—Mozart's *The Magic Flute?*—and the sound of hysterical sobbing coming from the living room. David noticed a vase of withering gladioli on the highboy flanking the entrance to the room.

Antonia shook the girl by the shoulders. "What happened, Mary? Where's Guy? *Where?*"

The girl was incoherent.

Gusts of wind blowing through the terrace doors made the curtains billow and the glass pendants on the chandeliers and wall sconces chime. Torino went outside to investigate.

The driving rain washed blood down the drain that was

imbedded in the tiled floor of the terrace. David's eyes traced the gory stream to its source, a curdled mass of white fur near the whiskey barrel that held a pine tree. It was the dog, Nanook. Dead.

He spotted something else a few paces away. He walked over and bent to pick up a soggy teddy bear. The stuffing of its stomach had been gouged out.

He scouted the terrace, searched the greenhouse. Nothing.

Emerging from the greenhouse on the eastern end of the terrace, he stopped, baffled, not wanting to think the unthinkable. His clothing was soaked.

Antonia appeared, face rigid, fists balled at her sides.

"He's not here," David said. "Did you look in the other rooms? What did Mary say?"

She shook her head. *"The eagle. The fucking eagle..."* She stared, mute, at the riotous sky.

ANTONIA stood in the streaming rain on the terra-cotta tiles where her son had been snatched away by the claws of the raptor.

Now her own claws were unsheathed.

She shifted her gaze from the sky to David's face. "Mary said it carried Guy off alive. *Alive.*"

They heard the front doorbell ring. They went back inside.

Bannister was at the door. "Where the hell have you been, Toni? I've left messages on your answering machine. I've got tremendous news." Then he noticed the stricken look on her face. "What's the matter?"

Torino told him.

"What?" It took a moment for the news to sink in.

"I think," Antonia said, "she did it as some kind of retribution for the death of her mate. We have to find the nest..."

"That's it," Bannister said. "We've found the nest. That's what I've been trying to tell you—"

"*Where?*"

"On the observation deck of the Woolworth Building. I saw it by accident when I was guiding the French delegates around the World Trade Center. One of them saw it through the binoculars."

"What're we waiting for?" said Torino, struggling into the sleeves of his trench coat.

"Hold *on*," said Bannister, heading for the hall telephone. "This takes some planning. The Mayor and Piccolo are waiting for us at Gracie Mansion. I'll tell them we're on our way."

The plan of action that emerged from the meeting at Gracie Mansion was based on the assumption that the child was still alive. Antonia had to believe it, and so had argued against using snipers out of fear that the bullets would hit the boy, who had been spotted by federal agents using a high-powered telescope from the sixtieth floor of the nearby Jacob Javits Office Building at twenty-six Federal Plaza. The eagle had been seen over the figure of the child. Observers also said that they thought they detected the child moving, although they couldn't be certain that the limbs weren't being moved by the activities of the mantling raptor. Some said police marksmen were skillful enough not to shoot the boy by mistake, but still the risk was too great. They compromised by posting snipers on surrounding rooftops and in nearby offices, but they were to fire their weapons only when and if the raptor flew from the nest. Antonia agreed but still worried about itchy trigger fingers.

Lokka had endorsed the strategy and made Antonia feel a little better when he said he believed the child was alive.

"What makes you think so?" asked Santiago, squinting at the scruffy-looking falconer.

"I know the bird. I know her like the palm of my hand.

She didn't kidnap the boy to kill him or eat him." His face, with its dry parchment skin, looked profoundly sad. "No. Not this time."

"Then why?" asked Torino.

Lokka seemed to weigh his words. "Many reasons, I think. First, it had something to do with her mate dying there. This was like a magnet drawing her to that terrace. But that's not all. I believe she's using the child as bait."

"Bait?" Torino said. "To catch what?"

"Me," Lokka replied.

LATER, oiling his piece and getting his gear ready, Torino puzzled over Lokka's remarks about how the eagle might be using the child as bait to set up a confrontation between herself and her former master and nemesis. It made, he guessed, a kind of lopsided sense. She was using a lure to tantalize the falconer, turning the tables on him, so to speak. Carrying on such thinking, one could say she somehow sensed she shared a destiny with the man who had taught *her* the art of predation, and whose child she had kidnapped almost a decade ago. And it was all brought to a head by the death of her mate. In her elemental way she associated the animal that had killed her mate with Raven Lokka, the representative of this outlandish species that she knew best.

Torino squinted down the barrel of his revolver, then holstered it. Pretty farfetched stuff, he told himself. What the hell did he know about the psychology of a raptor? Or Lokka either, for that matter. Trying to understand such things was like trying to grasp quicksilver.

IT was almost 10 P.M. when Chief Piccolo called the Special Operations Division to request they alert the Aviation Unit to provide two Jet Rangers a.s.a.p. Outside, the wind still

howled and heavy rains fell, prompting some talk of postponing the operation until morning when the storm was
expected to pass and daylight would make the job easier.
But they decided they couldn't risk waiting, in case the child
was still alive. When Torino volunteered to go up in one
helicopter Antonia insisted on going along. Each helicopter
would carry a sharpshooter. The second craft would hover
as a backup to the first. They must, they were reminded,
be careful not to frighten or provoke the bird into harming
the child. The feds offered Army Reserve helicopters but
Santiago said no. He wanted this to be a city operation. The
Interior Department Regional Director didn't press the matter, averting a jurisdictional squabble and protecting his rear
in the event of failure. They ruled out approaching the eyrie
by entering the building and going through the tower door,
again fearing she would harm the boy before they got to
her. Police would be posted by the tower door ready to rush
after—if—the raptor was lured into flight. Lokka said he
was sure that he could entice her into the air. Somehow
nobody doubted him. He had outlined the plan, moving
amid the ornate moldings and fluted furnishings of the mansion with a pantherlike grace and an air of competence.
Besides, he was, after all, the falconer, and knew this bird
like nobody else.

They drove out to Floyd Bennett Field in Bannister's official car, headlights splashing on the wet asphalt of Shore
Parkway. The Verrazano-Narrows Bridge was shrouded in
mist. Lokka sat up front with the driver. Antonia sat in the
back seat between Joe on her left and David on her right,
mismatched bookends. Alternating light and shadow pa-
raded over their faces as the car sped under the road lamps
toward the destination.

She turned to look straight ahead, fixing her attention on
the unwinding road that would lead them to the hangar
containing the helicopters that would carry them to the

copper mountain peak where her baby son was held captive, perhaps injured (near death?), certainly scared out of his wits.

Police Officer Arvin Taylor stood on the tarmac as the car pulled up to the hangar. He would serve as pilot of the chopper that would carry Lokka, Torino, and a police marksman. Antonia would fly in the backup helicopter.

Bannister pulled her aside. "There's really no reason for you to go up at all," he said.

"Don't try to stop me," she said.

"When this is over—" he began, but she cut him off.

"Please, Joe. Enough. It's no good, we both know it."

A howling wind coming off Jamaica Bay drowned out any answer. But of course he had none. He knew she was right.

The blades of the two helicopters on the tarmac began to chatter, stirring up a gale as she began to wade against the eddying air toward the backup helicopter. She noticed that David had been watching them from a distance, saw him turn away and climb aboard the first helicopter. She waved, put her head down and struggled on through the pitiless wind.

AFTER buckling his seat belt Torino gave a thumbs-up sign to the pilot. The craft lifted off, going slightly backward into the air like a housefly, then ascended into the turbulent sky. The detective adjusted the elastic band that secured his eyeglasses to his head and checked the chamber of his service revolver. He thought of his mother and her warnings, realized he was following the well-known proclivity of Italian sons to conjure mamma in moments of stress. Next thing he knew, he'd be making the sign of the cross.

The officer with the rifle sitting beside him, a bull-necked man, looked calm, almost bored. A hillbilly heading for a turkey shoot.

214

They had reached lower Manhattan. The buildings looked dark and fuzzy against the weltering sky, but Torino reckoned they must be somewhere near the Gothic tower of the Woolworth Building. Wisps of fog gauzed the chopper as it hovered in the wind. It was just after midnight. Taylor tilted the control column forward and pointed downward with his forefinger.

Torino focused his eyes, barely making out the sharp finial of the building below, the eyrie of the berkute. The lair.

The marksman released the safety on his rifle.

Lokka turned to the pilot. "Let's go down for a closer look."

Taylor glanced back at Torino, who nodded his assent. The pilot pushed down on the lever. The passengers' bodies shuddered in the hammering wind. The eggbeater descended. Crosswinds jabbered. Torino held his breath.

The eyrie had been built in the observation gallery just below the tower, festooned with architectural crags and crevices—spires, arches, flying buttresses and mocking gargoyles. The tower's portal braces made the peak of copper and steel impervious to the buffeting winds. Torino wished his nerves had been made of the same hard stuff.

It still was raining heavily.

The chopper came abreast of the observation gallery.

And there it was, insolent, imperial.

Where was the boy? Through the darkness Torino thought he could see a motionless, shadowy form. But was it Guy or just clumps of nesting material? Or carrion?

At the approach of the helicopter the eagle did not deign to raise her gold-crowned head.

Torino reviewed the plan Lokka had sketched out, less a well-defined strategy than an interrelated set of alternatives and fall-back positions. The first option called for Lokka getting near enough to the raptor to voice his familiar falconer's yell, hoping to entice it to fly toward him and thereby giving police enough time to rush out from the tower door and rescue the child before the eagle could fly back to the nest. Meanwhile the marksman would shoot the bird... Of course it was hardly certain that they'd find more than offal in the nest. But Torino fed on Antonia's hope. And clung to Lokka's conviction that the boy was still alive, even though deep down he doubted it. Manhattan was spread out like a dusky map below, streaked with streets, wriggling with traffic. Life throbbed and hummed down there. People clinked glasses and laughed. Bachelors climbed into sour unmade beds. David Torino, in the shivering steel carapace of the helicopter, high above all this, could only hope that the child's heart still pulsed like the city below.

Rain pounded the Woolworth Building. The berkute flounced her wings, making Torino wonder if she was aware of their presence nearby.

If for some reason the raptor did not respond to the falconer's call Torino was to act as a decoy. Wearing a bulletproof vest under his shirt and leather gloves and fencing mask provided by Lokka, he would descend by nylon ladder to the deck on the opposite side of the nest and try to draw her away from the child. Then, if possible without endangering his own or the child's life, he was supposed to shoot the creature with a tranquilizer. In spite of Lokka's strong opposition, federal authorities who lived by the book still preferred taking the berkute alive, for scientific reasons, they said. Of course they all agreed the first priority was saving the boy. Antonia—a scientist in theory, an enraged mother in fact—agreed with *that*. The marksmen posted on surrounding parapets, rooftops, and in office windows as well as on the two helicopters were assigned to back him up, but they would be of little use in this fog even though the tower was illuminated as usual to show off its architectural details.

Brunhild, still mantling over the huddled form of what was presumably the child in the nest in the center of the observation gallery, seemed to puff up her thorax like an affronted grande dame. Was she acknowledging their presence? Torino wondered. And all the while he couldn't help marvelling at her great size and imposing beauty.

The helicopter hovered some twenty feet from the railing of the observation deck, and now Torino could see clearly enough to tell that the form in the nest indeed *was* the boy. The body stirred. *He was still alive.*

They radioed Antonia in the backup helicopter to tell her.

Then Lokka turned around and stared at Torino. It was a wordless signal that the operation was about to begin. Torino swallowed hard. Suddenly he recalled a scrap of poetry from his high school days—the Jesuits made wayward boys memorize lines of verse before releasing them from detention. They were from Shelley's "Prometheus" . . .

Pour forth heaven's wine, Indaean Ganymede,
And let it fill the Daedal cups like fire.

He devoutly hoped that the wine in this case would not be the little boy's blood—and then he saw Lokka lean out of the helicopter door, cup his mouth and utter the other-worldly, high-pitched falconer's call.

Twenty-nine

As LOKKA UTTERED the familiar ululant sound, he felt for the first time in a long time acutely alive.

The rain muttered. The helicopter rocked in the roiling air. Lokka squinted into the shadows, trying to make out Brunhild's reaction to his call. He saw her only raise her primaries and crane her head from one side to the other. It had been a long time since she last heard it. He cupped his mouth again.

This time when the sound reached her she gingerly stepped a few paces away from the nest. How did this reminder of her liaison—bondage—make her feel? Did she have such feelings? Lokka was convinced that she did.

The fog thickened and Lokka's flesh felt clammy. He thought about Jack and Iris. And he thought about Ali Kanat. It was an effort to conjure them up, shrouded as they were in the fog of memory. And strangely, they seemed now almost irrelevant to what was taking place nearly eight-hundred feet in the air over the city.

This was between him and the berkute.

As the craft wavered in the wind he momentarily lost sight of the raptor behind a buttress attached to the rail of the gallery and extending up the tower. He turned to the pilot, who seemed worried by the savagery of the winds. "Can't we get just a little closer?"

Taylor shook his head. "Don't want to take the chance of my tail sideswiping the tower. Having a hard enough time controlling this baby—"

Suddenly from the back seat Torino shouted, "Look!"

The eagle was flying from the gallery, a wriggling bundle in her talons. She banked around, ascended a few feet and deposited the hostage on an inaccessible ledge just below the finial. Again she brooded over the child in what seemed to Lokka's eyes a protective way. Threatened by possible predators, she had taken the nestling to a higher crag on the mountain peak. Lokka gazed in something like awe at this strange rite staged by nature in the cathedral-like setting of the Woolworth tower.

"What's she doing?" asked Torino.

"Protecting her eyass from this big alien bird," Lokka said. Not like with Jack, he thought bitterly.

The marksman shouldered the rifle.

Torino put a hand on his arm and shook his head. "You think the kid is in danger of falling?" he asked Lokka.

"Don't think so, the ledge is pretty wide. And it's protected by some sort of stone fretting." Lokka tried calling again, but the sound, apparently muted now by the storm, had no effect. Then a few seconds later the bird unexpectedly glided back down to the observation deck, seemingly confused, or ambivalent.

Torino shouted to the pilot, "Now, quick, hover over the ledge where the kid is and I'll let down the ladder."

The pilot nodded as he manipulated the lever and control column. But as he maneuvered the helicopter into position the bird soared off into the low-hanging weltering clouds.

By now Taylor had jockeyed the chopper into a hover position some twenty feet above the ledge. He could not get closer without risking hitting the spire. "Let's work fast," Torino said as he untied the ladder and threw it overboard, then watched as it seesawed in the strong wind.

"I'm coming with you," said Lokka.

Torino nodded, took a deep breath before climbing out of the helicopter into the raging night sky. Lokka, the dagger fixed in his garrison belt, followed right behind him.

As they descended the swinging ladder, the bottom of which kept losing contact with the ledge, the rain and wind lashed their bodies like a scourge. They were close enough now to hear the child crying. Lokka had to stop and wait because the windswept ladder was pitching so much Torino could not get a secure footing on the ledge. The falconer glanced up at the pilot to shout something but what he saw made the words catch in his throat.

Through the mist fell the great eagle at the end of a headlong dive, wings half-closed, plummeting like a stone, spinning like a bullet, heading for the tilted chopper. Bracing himself, Lokka tried to shout a warning to Torino.

The bird struck the side of the helicopter like a tidal wave, jarring the two men loose from the ladder and spinning the aircraft in the flailing winds.

Lokka felt himself hurtling through the sky and tumbling onto a circular landing of the building just above the portal braces that rose from the observation gallery. He had fallen only about ten feet, and when he moved gingerly, he found he was unhurt. He glowered at a couple of copper spires nearby that might have impaled him if he had fallen a few feet to the other side. He wondered about Torino. He had been very close to the ledge. Had he made it?

Hugging the slanted wall brace with his back, the falconer got to his feet and looked up. The helicopter, after wobbling, had regained equilibrium and hovered to the south. Apparently the marksmen had held off shooting the eagle out of fear of hitting the rotors.

Where was she now?

There. She swooped upward again, vanishing into the skeins of cloud and mist, but Lokka was sure in his gut that she would return, and soon. His cadaverous face glistened with rain. The creature was possessed, he believed. And what was he?

He tried to halloo to the aircraft but it was no use.

The eagle struck again, this time hitting the section of the ship near the tail rotor. The copter spun around like a runaway eggbeater. Lokka could do nothing but watch as it began to spin in the opposite direction of the main rotor, caught in the maelstrom of torque. The craft dipped, hit the side of a building and burst into flames.

Dodging cross-cuts of rifle fire, the berkute vanished again.

Feeling impatient, Lokka realized that Brunhild might well return to her eyrie now that the big bird that had threatened her was killed.

Good. He *wanted* her to come. He heard the dim clatter of the backup helicopter that carried Antonia. Otherwise the night was relatively quiet now, the storm having abated. Again he cupped his mouth and uttered the falconer's call.

In an instant he heard the thunder of her wingbeat. Her familiar musky scent assailed his nostrils. And then she was right there, before him, with her glassy stare and arched beak.

He drew the curved *kukri* from his belt.

She hovered over the landing, blotting out the emerging moon.

But suddenly she sheared off, made a short twisting ascent

and circled the ledge where the child lay. Lokka cursed and called out again.

Somewhere from above he heard her *squark* and flutter her wings again. His face was flushed. A light shining from inside the tower cast a greenish glow over the gothic carvings of the facade.

Lokka braced himself and waited.

She appeared before him, hovering in the air. He could see her clearly. The dull yellow cere around the black beak, the concentric circles of the cornea, pupil and brown iris of her right eye. He could feel her breath on him. He saw uncased her veiny yellow toes and black claws, the golden lanceolate plumage, the finery she wore to greet him. And he saw her black slithery tongue. All these images registered on his brain in the instant before she spread her amber arms like a lover to pinion him in her praying-mantis embrace.

She slammed into him, knocking him down. With the impact, her wings clattered like wooden slats in a gale wind. Lokka flogged her with the knife. She flashed her beak, uttering a muffled bark, trying to bind the victim's nose and suffocate him. He screamed, plunging the knife into her just as her talons gored their way through leather and flesh.

Locked together, tumbling and turning in the air, they fell from the ledge. Just before oblivion curtained the falconer's eyes, he thought of Iris and little Jack. And then there was nothing at all.

TORINO had fallen hard on his right side, striking the copper brace. He bounced once and landed on his face. He lay there stunned for a full minute before trying to move. As he tested his muscles and limbs pain knifed his right rib cage and hip. A sweet sticky liquid trickled down his right cheek into his mouth. His fingers groped toward his face. The lenses of his eyeglasses were smashed to bits.

He staggered to his feet, realized he was standing on some sort of flat surface, probably the roof of the observation gallery. The glare seemed to come from the tower light that stood like a lighthouse beacon behind vaulted windows near the apex of the building. The presence of the light in some ways made it even more difficult for him to see what he was doing. In a moment his eyes adjusted some and he could see a little better.

He heard a great commotion in the sky above him.

He shielded his eyes and squinted in the direction of the sound. Was the eagle attacking the helicopter? Soon came the sound of a tremendous crash and the night sky fulminated with garish orange color.

He slumped to the roof-surface, catching his breath, trying to collect his emotions, fighting panic, pain searing his side.

He heard the falconer cry out.

It had come from somewhere right beneath him. So Lokka had survived and was calling to the raptor. And what, he wondered, would that lunatic do if she answered his call?

Her stench hit his senses first, then the clatter of her wings. Fear took away his breath, but his body pulsed with adrenalin.

She was somewhere nearby.

A shadow fell over him, then vanished. Momentary relief. From under his down vest he drew out the service revolver. She seemed to be hovering just one tier below on the crusty green wedding-cake tower, where Lokka apparently had fallen. The sound of her wingbeat suddenly grew louder; his hand tensed on the pistol grip. The huge bird circled where he stood but he couldn't see well enough to draw a bead on her. It would take a very well-aimed bullet to bring this monster down, he realized.

Again she flew out of sight.

He crawled under a buttress to the edge of the roof, stationed himself between two sharp gables and peered below. Through the lifting fog, darkness, and myopia he could make out the blurred outlines of the death struggle. The body of the man and beast had merged into one griffonlike form, a hybrid to rival any gargoyle on the lace-in-stone structure that served as a backdrop to their coupling. A blade scintillated in the shadows. Then, soundlessly, the yoked combatants plunged to the parapets below.

Silence. Torino felt like a witness to some primeval event. Then he heard the ruckus of the backup helicopter's rotors coming nearer. At least Antonia was safe.

He called out, struggled to his feet and waved his arms, but couldn't tell if the occupants saw or heard him.

The aircraft made a few passes around the building and finally came sufficiently close that Torino thought he saw Antonia waving at him from inside the helicopter. But again they couldn't seem to get close enough to rescue the child without hitting the structure. He heard whimpering, and as he looked up he thought he saw the boy's leg dangling from the circular ledge that surrounded the finial of the tower.

If Guy moved even slightly he was in danger of falling off the ledge.

Torino wasted no more time. He had no choice. He had to try to reach the boy by climbing up the structural features of the building. As well as he could he traced the moldings, carvings, crockets, piers, buttresses, ribs, vaults and gables that lay between him and Guy. Thank God the structure was so richly ornamented. He judged the distance between them to be about fifteen or twenty feet. He stripped off his down vest, bulletproof vest, and holster. He spat on his hands. For the most part, he realized, he would have to rely on his sense of touch. And physical strength. From his lightheadedness he sensed that he had lost a fair amount of blood. Well, he would have to tap the reserve tank.

Taking a deep breath, he started by shimmying up a sloping buttress, slick with rain and perspiration from his hands. He tried to blot out thoughts of failure from his mind as he inched upward.

Finally he reached the end of the structural element, gasping for breath. He rested, then extended his hand as high as he could and touched a circular horizontal base ornamented with recessed cinquefoils that might give him a purchase to lift himself up to the ledge. He hesitated, struggling against a rush of fear, then gripped the tracery and began to lift himself off the buttress.

A gust of wind rose up.

His left hand slipped off the molding. He held on by his right hand, his feet kicking in the air. His fingers were raw and bleeding. Slipping. Straining every muscle in his shoulder, he managed to hold on until his left hand found another recess in the tracery and he pulled himself up to the ledge. He lay with his head on the hard surface, gulping in air. He couldn't believe he had made it—

He heard a terrified cry.

He looked up and saw Guy reacting to the grunting apparition with blood-streaked face that was now David Torino.

He did what he could to reassure the boy, make him realize who it was, then reached out to shelter him in his arms.

The rattling of the chopper blades filled his ears as he waited for them to get the boy and himself off this godforsaken tower.

Thirty

UNDER A BRASSY noon sun the male red panda waddled over to the hollow log and rubbed his lower parts on it.

Guy tugged the sleeve of Torino's khaki coat. "What's he doing?"

Torino consulted the brochure printed by the New York Zoological Society describing Buddha, the new mate for Lucy obtained from the *wah*-breeding program at a conservation and research center in Virginia. It said that he was leaving "scent posts" to warn off other males (even though May was too late in the mating season for conception to occur). How was he going to explain this to Guy?

"I think he's got an itch," was the best he could come up with.

And speaking of itches, Torino had a monster one under the bandages that swathed his rib cage, but the four fractured ribs made his side too sore to scratch properly. He

226

also had some cuts and bruises on his face but they were almost healed.

He squeezed Guy's hand. "How about an ice cream?"

This was his first time out since getting over a bout with pneumonia. "You bet," he said.

Before leaving they took a last look at the panda enclosure. Buddha was shadowing Lucy, nuzzling her tail. She flicked her tail and then scampered off. Guy laughed, giving Torino the distinct impression that the kid knew more about the birds and bees than he let on.

When it came right down to it, Torino reflected as they moved down the wooden walkway, who really knew anything about the bees and birds? Especially the birds. Why had Brunhild kidnapped Guy? Maybe to lure Lokka into a confrontation. Maybe not. Why hadn't she harmed him? The experts fumbled for answers. Maybe it had been nothing much more complicated than plain old maternal instinct. That was Torino's theory.

The bodies of the berkute and Lokka had been found as though fused together on a terrace of the Woolworth Building. She had disemboweled him. He had plunged the knife into her thorax, striking the heart. In death the falconer's face had a look of near-serenity. Nature always had tricks up her sleeve.

Torino shaded the face of his wristwatch from the rays of the sun. "Finish up, kid," he said. "Time to go meet your mother."

They hopped a Fifth Avenue bus heading downtown. Torino fidgeted in the seat; his injuries made it hard for him to find a comfortable position. Still, he smiled, counted himself damn lucky even to have survived. Through the window he saw a pedestrian brandish his fist at a bicycle messenger. Ah, spring in New York. It felt good to be alive. He thought about this crazy city, no longer panic-stricken.

The celestial terror was over; the usual terrestrial terrors remained.

He supposed that the French World's Fair delegation had hopped the Concorde by now. They had promised a quick decision, according to Bannister. Who cared? New Yorkers staged an exposition every day of the year.

Of course Bannister cared. But Torino was surprised at how he'd backed off without a fight when Antonia broke off their relationship. Well, he and Bannister were cut from a different cloth.

Torino gazed out of the bus window. Throngs of office workers in shirt sleeves and light cotton clothes lunched *al fresco*, perched on parapets of fountains and plazas of concrete and stone. A four-piece band played Dixieland and passed the hat around. He blinked at the sight of a flock of pigeons swirling around the head of Prometheus in Rockefeller Center. Birds. People hardly noticed them, took them for granted. He never would again.

When the bus got to the corner of Forty-second Street Torino and the boy got off and walked west in the direction of the CUNY Graduate Center. A panhandler stuck out his hand. The child, imitating pro athletes, slapped it. Torino gave the man a dollar, not forgetting Casey.

In the elevator he checked his right pocket for the Mets tickets. There they were, good seats, too, right on the first-base line and not too far from the dugout. A cop did get a few perks. Maybe he'd pop the question during the seventh inning stretch.

Whoa, slow down.

They sat in the rear of the lecture hall. Guy's mouth was circled like a clown's with chocolate. Torino really enjoyed the boy. Antonia? Give her time. After what she'd been through... There would be the Met game tonight, dinner Friday, a play next Wednesday. And she had asked to be with him the following Sunday when he would receive a commendation at a police-headquarters ceremony to be attended by the Mayor (and his press secretary?).

Antonia was nearing the conclusion of her lecture on the subject of raptors. She could still talk about them. In spite of the trouble she'd been through, she still had her feeling for birds, including even raptors. Man, she had said, was the real raptor, the one who fouled the waters, poisoned the air, disfigured the forests. He was sure she still believed this. After all, hadn't a man-made disaster, Chernobyl, probably been responsible for the mutant Brunhild? Of course, if anything had happened to Guy, she admitted, she would hardly have been able to be so objective. For the scientist also belonged to the female of the species *homo sapiens* variety—mother. A wonder of nature, Torino thought, smiling as she walked down the aisle toward him.

Not far away a peregrine falcon beats her long wings rapidly, flying south from her roost in the golden dome of the Metropolitan Life tower on east Twenty-third Street. The notched-beak bird soars with great speed and purpose, following a mysterious instinct through the concrete canyons of Manhattan toward the Woolworth Building.

With a flurry of wings she lands on the outdoor observatory and pads over to the detritus of the berkute's nest. She pokes her bobbing beak through the large dry sticks, decorative duck feathers, leafy sprigs of fir trees and other material gleaned from the bosky fringes of the city until she finds what some internal radar had told her was there.

TALONS

The bird climbs astride the object, spreading her bones and feathers over it. She is not ruffled by its large size or slightly alien form. She broods contentedly on the egg, a white thing blotched with brown spots. She adopts it as her own.

**INDEXED IN
STACKS FICTION**